Michael Hague's Favourite Hans Christian Andersen Fairy Tales

Michael Hague's Favourite Hans Christian Andersen Fairy Tales

HOLT, RINEHART AND WINSTON
NEW YORK

TO THE MEMORY OF JOHN WINFIELD BURDICK

Published by Holt, Rinehart and Winston, 383 Madison Avenue, New York, New York, 10017.

Published simultaneously in Canada by Holt, Rinehart and Winston of Canada, Limited.

Library of Congress Catalog Card Number: 81-47455
ISBN: 0-03-059528-2

Printed in the United States of America
3 5 7 9 10 8 6 4 2

Offset Printing and Binding: Krueger, New Berlin, Wisconsin
Color Separations: Offset Separations Corporation, Turin, Italy
Composition: Waldman Graphics, Pennsauken, New Jersey

Designer: Marc Cheshire
Editorial Production: Jill Weinstein
Production: Karen Gillis

Contents

❧ The Snow Queen ❧

FIRST STORY

The Mirror and the Broken Pieces

ALL RIGHT NOW, we're going to begin. When we come to the end of the story we shall know more than we do now, for he was a bad goblin! He was one of the very worst, for he was the devil. One day he was in a very good humour, for he had made a mirror that had this peculiarity: everything good and beautiful that was reflected in it shrank into almost nothing, while all that was worthless and ugly was magnified and looked even worse than before. The most lovely landscapes looked like boiled spinach and the nicest people looked hideous, or stood on their heads and had no bodies. Their faces were so distorted that no one would know them, and people's freckles spread all over their noses and mouths. That was most amusing, said the devil. When a good or pious thought passed through anyone's mind, it was shown in the mirror in such an ugly way that the devil chuckled at his cleverness. All who went to the goblin school—for he ran a goblin school—declared it was a miracle. For at last, they asserted, one could see for the first time how the world and the people in it really looked. They ran to the ends of the world with the mirror, until at last there was not a country or a person that had not been seen distorted in it. Next they wanted to fly up to heaven with it, to scoff at the angels and the Lord Himself. The

I

higher they flew with the mirror, the worse it grinned, until they could scarcely hold it. Higher and higher they flew, nearer to God and the angels, and then the mirror trembled so much that it slipped out of their hands and fell to earth, where it shattered into a hundred million billion splinters, or perhaps even more. That caused a greater misfortune than before, for some of the splinters were no bigger than a grain of sand and were scattered all over the world. Whenever they flew into anyone's eye, they stuck there and made the person see everything distorted, for every fragment had retained the same power as the whole mirror. Some people even got a tiny splinter of the mirror in their hearts, and that was terrible, for such a heart became a block of ice. A few pieces of the glass were so large that they were used as windowpanes, but it was bad to look at one's friends through these panes. Other pieces were made into glasses, and when people put on these glasses to see correctly and fairly, things went all wrong. Then the Evil One laughed till his paunch shook; it delighted him so. But some fragments of glass still floated in the air.

SECOND STORY

A Little Boy and a Little Girl

In the big town where there are so many houses and people that there isn't room enough for everyone to have a little garden, and where most people must therefore be content with flowers in flowerpots, there lived two poor children who had a garden somewhat bigger than a flowerpot. They weren't brother and sister, but they loved each other almost as much as if they had been. Their parents lived next to each other, in two garrets, where the roof of one neighbour's house joined that of the other, with the gutter running between them. In each house was a little window. All you had to do to get from one window to the other was to step across the gutter.

Outside each window the parents had placed a big wooden box, in which they grew the vegetables they used and a little rose bush; there was one rose bush in each box, and they grew beautifully. One day the parents decided to place the boxes across the gutter, so that they nearly reached from one window to another and looked just like two walls of flowers. Sweet peas hung over the boxes, and the rose bushes sent out long shoots, which clustered around the windows and bent towards each other. It was almost like a triumphal arch of flowers and leaves. Because the boxes were very high and the children knew that they must not climb on them, they were often allowed to go out onto the roof behind the boxes and sit on their stools under the roses. There they could play to their heart's content.

Winter brought an end to this amusement. The windows often frosted over. But then the children warmed coins on the stove and held them against the frosted pane. This made a lovely round peephole. And out of each, peeped a bright friendly eye, one from each window; it was the little boy and the little girl. His name was Kay and hers was Gerda.

In the summer they could get to each other in one jump, but in the winter they had to go down and up many stairs, while the snow was falling outside.

"It is the white bees that are swarming," said the old grandmother.

"Do they also have a queen bee?" asked the little boy, for he knew each hive had one.

"Yes, they do," said the grandmother. "She always flies where they swarm thickest. She is the largest of them all and never settles on the earth, but flies up again into the black sky. Many a winter's night she flies through the streets of the town and looks in the windows, and then they freeze immediately and look like flowers."

"Yes, I've seen that," both the children said, and so they knew that it was true.

"Can the Snow Queen come in here?" asked the little girl.

"Let her try!" said the boy. "I'll put her on the hot stove, and then she'll melt."

But the grandmother smoothed his hair, and told them some more tales.

In the evening when Kay was at home and half undressed, he climbed up on the chair by the window and looked out through the little hole. A few flakes of snow were falling outside, and one of them, the largest of all, settled on the edge of one of the flower boxes. The snowflake grew larger and larger, until at last it became a maiden clothed in the finest white gauze made of millions of star-like flakes. She was beautiful and delicate, but of ice—of blinding, sparkling ice. Yet she was alive; her eyes flashed like two bright stars, but there was no peace or rest in them. She nodded towards the window and beckoned with her hand. The little boy was frightened and jumped down from the chair, and at the same moment it seemed as if a large bird flew by outside the window.

Next day it was clear and frosty. Then came the thaw, and with it the spring. The sun shone, the green shoots appeared, the swallows built their nests, the windows were opened, and the little children sat in their garden again, high up on the roof, at the top of the house.

How beautifully the roses bloomed that summer! The little girl had learned a hymn in which there was something about roses, which made her think of her own roses. So she sang it to the little boy, and he sang too:

> Roses fade and die, but we
> Our Infant Lord shall surely see.

And the two children held each other's hands, kissed the roses, and looked up at God's bright sunshine and spoke to it, as if the Christ-child were there. What lovely summer days those were! How beautiful it was out there, by the sweet rose bushes, which seemed as if they would never stop blooming!

Kay and Gerda sat and looked at the picture book of beasts and birds. It was then, exactly as the clock struck five in the great church tower, that Kay said:

"Oh! Something has stabbed my heart! And now something has got into my eye!"

The little girl put her arms around his neck. He blinked his eyes. But no, there was nothing at all to be seen.

"I think it is gone," said he. But it was not gone. It was one of those splinters of glass from the mirror—the goblin's mirror that we remember so well, the ugly glass that made everything great and good seem small and hideous, while the mean and the wicked things became distinct and large, and every fault could be seen at once. Poor little Kay had also received a splinter right in his heart, which would soon become like a lump of ice. It did not hurt him anymore, but the splinter was still there.

"Why are you crying?" he asked. "You look ugly like that. There's nothing the matter with me. Oh, look!" he cried suddenly. "That rose is worm-eaten, and this one is crooked! They're ugly roses, after all—like the box they stand in!"

And he kicked the box with his foot and tore off both of the roses.

"Kay, what are you doing?" cried the little girl.

And seeing her dismay, he tore off another rose and jumped in through his own window, away from dear little Gerda.

Afterwards, when she came with her picture book, he said it was only fit for babies. When Grandmother told stories, he was always sure to put in a *but*. Whenever he could he would get behind her, put on a pair of glasses, and imitate her, which he did perfectly, and people laughed at him. Soon he could mimic the voice and walk of everybody in the street. Everything that was peculiar or ugly about them Kay would imitate. And people said, "He must certainly have a remarkable head, that boy!" But it was the glass that had gotten into his eye, the glass that had lodged in his heart, that made him do it, and even made him tease little Gerda, who loved him with all her heart.

His games now became quite different from what they had been before. They became quite serious and sensible. One winter's day, when the snow was falling, he came out with a magnifying glass, held up the tail of his blue coat, and let the snowflakes fall upon it.

"Now look through the glass, Gerda," he said.

Every flake of snow was magnified and looked like a lovely flower or a star with ten points; it was beautiful to behold.

"Look!" said Kay. "They're much more interesting than real flowers. They're perfect, until they begin to melt."

Soon after Kay came out wearing thick gloves, and with his sled on his back. He shouted into Gerda's ears, "I've got permission to go into the main square, where the other boys play." And off he went.

In the big square the boldest boys often tied their sleds to the country people's carts and were pulled along a good way with them. It was great fun. At the height of their game a big sled came along. It was painted red with white markings, and in it sat somebody wrapped in a rough white fur and wearing a rough white cap. The sled drove twice around the square, and Kay managed to fasten his little sled to it, and away he went. It went faster and faster, straight into the next street. The driver turned around and nodded in a friendly way to Kay, as if they knew each other. Every time Kay wanted to cast loose his sled, the stranger nodded again, and so Kay stayed where he was, until at last they drove out through the town gate. Then the snow began to fall so fast that the boy could not see his hand in front of him, but still on he went. Then he finally dropped the rope, to get loose from the big sled, but it was no use, for his little sled was bound fast to the other, and on they went like the wind. Then he called out loudly, but nobody heard him; and the snow fell fast and the sled flew on. Every now and then it gave a jump, and they seemed to be flying over hedges and ditches. The boy was terribly frightened. He wanted to say his prayers, but all he could remember were the multiplication tables.

The snowflakes became larger and larger, until at last they looked like big white birds. All at once they flew aside and the big sled stopped, and the person who had driven it stood up. The fur and the cap were made of snow. It was a lady, so tall and slender, all glittering white! It was the Snow Queen.

"We have travelled fast!" she said. "But you are shivering with cold! Creep under my bearskin."

And she put him beside her in her own sled and wrapped the fur around him. He felt as if he were sinking into a snowdrift.

"Are you still cold?" she asked, and then she kissed him on the forehead.

Ugh! That kiss was colder than ice; it went right through to his heart, half of which was already a lump of ice. He felt as if he were going to die, but only for a moment. Then he felt fine again, and did not notice the cold anymore.

"My sled! Don't forget my sled!"

That was the first thing he thought of, for it was fastened to one of the white fowls that flew behind them with the sled on its back. The Snow Queen kissed Kay once more, and then he forgot little Gerda, and his grandmother, and everyone at home.

"Now you shall have no more kisses," she said, "for I could kiss you to death."

Kay looked at her. She was so beautiful; he could not imagine a wiser or more lovely face. She did not appear to be made of ice now, as she had when she had sat outside the window and beckoned to him. In his eyes she was perfect; he did not feel afraid at all. He told her he could do arithmetic up to fractions, and that he knew

the number of square miles and the population of all the countries. And as he talked she smiled. It seemed to him that what he knew was not enough, and he looked up into the vast, endless space, and she flew with him high up on the black cloud, and a storm blew and whistled. It seemed as though the wind sang old songs. They flew over forests and lakes, over land and sea. Beneath them the cold wind roared, the wolves howled, the snow glistened; above them black screaming crows flew, but above all the moon shone bright and clear, and Kay gazed at it through the long, long winter night. By day he slept at the feet of the Snow Queen.

THIRD STORY

The Flower Garden of the Woman Who Knew Magic

But what did Gerda think when Kay did not return? No one knew what had really happened to him. The boys could only say that they had seen him tie his sled to another very large one, which had driven along the street and out through the town gate. Nobody knew what had become of him. Many tears were shed, and little Gerda cried long and bitterly. Then they said he was dead—he had drowned in the river that flowed by the town. Oh, those were long dark winter days! Then spring came, with its warm sunshine.

"Kay is dead and gone," said little Gerda.

"I don't believe it," said the sunshine.

"He is dead and gone," said she to the swallows.

"We don't believe it," they replied, until finally Gerda did not believe it herself.

"I will take my new red shoes," she said one morning, "the ones that Kay has never seen, and I will go down to the river and ask it about him."

It was still very early. She kissed the grandmother, who was still asleep, took her red shoes, and went all alone through the town gate down to the river.

"Is it true that you have taken my friend? I will make you a present of my red shoes if you will give him back to me!"

And it seemed to her as if the waves nodded strangely; and then she took her red shoes, which she liked more than anything she owned, and threw them into the river. But they fell close to the bank, and the little waves washed them back to land again. It seemed as if the river would not take from her the dearest things she had, because it didn't have her friend Kay. But she simply thought she had not thrown the shoes out far enough, so she climbed into a boat that lay among the reeds, went to the farther end of the boat, and threw the shoes into the water again. The boat was not made fast, however, and her movement caused it to drift away from the shore. She noticed it and hurried to get back, but before she reached the other end of the boat it was a yard from the bank and was floating quickly away.

Then Gerda was very frightened and began to cry, but no one heard her except the sparrows, and they could not carry her to land. They flew along the bank and sang, as if to console her, "Here we are! Here we are!" The boat drifted downstream and little Gerda sat quite still in her stockings. Her little red shoes floated along behind, but they could not catch up with the boat, which drifted faster.

It was very pretty on both sides. There were beautiful flowers, old trees, and slopes with sheep and cows, but not a human being was to be seen anywhere.

"Perhaps the river will carry me to little Kay," thought Gerda. Then she became more cheerful, and stood up, and for many hours she watched the pretty green banks. At last she came to a big cherry orchard, where there was a little house with curious blue and red windows. It had a thatched roof, and in front stood two wooden soldiers, who presented arms to those who sailed past.

Gerda called out to them, for she thought they were alive, but, of course, they couldn't answer. The river carried the boat in towards the shore.

Gerda called out still louder, and then out of the house came an old, old woman leaning on a crutch. She had on a big sun hat painted with the loveliest flowers.

"You poor child!" said the old woman. "How did you manage to come on the great river and to float so far out into the wide world?"

And then the old woman waded into the water, hooked the boat with her crutch, drew it to land, and lifted Gerda out. Gerda was glad to be on dry land again, though she felt a little afraid of the strange old woman.

"Come and tell me who you are and how you got here," she said. And Gerda told her everything. The old woman shook her head and said, "Hm! hm!" Gerda asked her if she had seen Kay. The woman said no, that he had not yet come by, but that he probably would come soon. In any case, Gerda shouldn't feel sad, but should taste her cherries and look at the flowers, for they were better than any picture book: each one of them could tell a story. Then she

took Gerda by the hand and led her into the little house, and the old woman locked the door after them.

The windows were very high, and the panes were red, blue, and yellow, so that the daylight shone in in a strange many-coloured way. On the table stood the finest cherries, and Gerda ate as many as she liked, for she had been told she could. While she was eating them the old woman combed Gerda's hair with a golden comb, and her hair curled and shone like lovely gold around her sweet little face, which was round and as blooming as a rose.

"I have long wished for a dear little girl like you," said the old woman. "Now you will see how well we shall get on together."

And the more she combed Gerda's hair, the more Gerda forgot her playmate Kay, for this old woman could work magic, though she was not a wicked witch. She only dabbled in a little magic for her own amusement, and now only because she wanted to keep little Gerda. She went into the garden, pointed her crutch towards all the rose bushes, and, beautiful as they were, they all sank into the black earth, until no one could tell where they had stood. The old woman was afraid that if Gerda saw roses she would think of her own, remember Kay, and run away.

Then she took Gerda out into the flower garden. Every flower you could think of was there in full bloom, not only spring flowers, but summer and autumn flowers too, and their lovely fragrance filled the air. No picture book could be gayer and prettier. Gerda jumped for joy, and played until the sun went down behind the tall cherry trees. Then she was put into a lovely bed with red silk pillows stuffed with blue violets, and she slept there, and dreamed as happily as a queen on her wedding day.

Next day she played again with the flowers in the warm sunshine, and so many days went by. Gerda got to know every flower, but it always seemed to her that one was missing, though which one it was she didn't know. One day she sat looking at the old woman's sun hat with the painted flowers, and it so happened that the prettiest of them all was a rose. The old woman had forgotten to remove it from her hat when she made the other roses sink into the ground.

"What, are there no roses here?" cried Gerda.

She went among the flower beds and searched and searched, but there was not one rose to be found. Then she sat down and cried, and her hot tears fell just upon a spot where a rose tree lay buried. When the warm tears moistened the earth, the tree shot up again, as blooming as when it had sunk. Gerda kissed the roses, thought of the beautiful ones at home, and with them of little Kay.

"Oh, how I have been wasting my time!" said the little girl. "I who ought to have been looking for Kay! Do you know where he is?" she asked the roses. "Do you think he is dead?"

"He is not dead," said the roses. "We have been in the ground. All the dead people are there, but Kay isn't there."

"Thank you," said Gerda. She went to the other flowers, looked into their cups, and asked, "Do you not know where Kay is?"

Every flower stood in the sun, thinking only of her own story or fairy tale. Little Gerda heard many of them, but not one knew anything of Kay.

And what did the tiger lily say?

"Do you hear the drum go rub-a-dub? There are only three notes, always rub-a-dub! Hear the funeral chant of the women! Hear the call of the priests! The Hindu woman stands in her long red robe on the funeral pile. The flames rise up around her and her dead husband; but the Hindu woman is thinking of the living one here in the circle, of him whose eyes burn hotter than flames, whose glances burn in her soul more ardently than the flames themselves which are soon to burn her body to ashes. Can the flame of the heart die in the flames of the funeral pile?"

"I don't understand that at all!" said little Gerda.

"That is my story," said the tiger lily.

What does the morning glory say?

"Over the narrow mountain path hangs an old knight's castle. The ivy grows thick over the crumbling red walls, leaf by leaf up to the balcony, and there stands a beautiful girl. She leans over the balustrade and gazes up the path. No rose on its stem is fresher than she, no apple blossom wafted by the wind floats more lightly along. How her costly silks rustle! 'Will he never come?' "

"Is it Kay you mean?" asked little Gerda.

"I am only talking of my own story—my dream," replied the morning glory.

What did the little snowdrop say?

"Between two trees a board is hanging on ropes: it is a swing. Two pretty little girls, with dresses as white as snow and green silk ribbons on their hats, are sitting on it, swinging. Their brother, who is bigger than they are, stands on the swing with his arm around the rope to hold himself, for in one hand he has a little bowl, and in the other a clay pipe: he is blowing soap bubbles. The swing moves, and the bubbles fly up with beautiful changing colours; the last one still hangs from the bowl of the pipe, swayed by the wind. The swing moves to and fro. A little black dog, light as the bubbles, stands up on its hind legs and wants to be taken onto the swing. It goes on, and the dog falls, and barks with anger: the bubble bursts. A swinging board and a shimmering foam picture—that is my song!"

"It may be very pretty, but you speak so sadly, and you don't mention little Kay at all."

What do the hyacinths say?

"There were three beautiful sisters, transparent and delicate. One's dress was red, the second blue, and the third pure white. Hand in hand they danced by the calm lake in the bright moonlight. They were not elves, but of humans born. It was so sweet and fragrant there! The girls disappeared in the forest, and the fragrance became sweeter still. Three coffins, with the three beautiful maidens lying in them, glided from the thicket across the lake. The fireflies flew around them like little hovering lights. Are the dancing girls sleeping, or are they dead? The flower scent says they are dead. The evening bell tolls their knell!"

"You make me very sad," said Gerda. "Your scent is so strong, I can't help thinking of the dead maidens. Ah! is Kay really dead? The roses have been down under the ground, and they say no."

"Ding, dong!" rang the hyacinth bells. "We are not tolling for little Kay—we do not know him. We only sing our song, the only one we know."

And Gerda went to the buttercup, shining out among the green leaves.

"You are a little bright sun," said Gerda. "Tell me, if you know—where shall I find my friend?"

The buttercup shone gaily, and looked back at Gerda. What song could the buttercup sing? It was not about Kay.

"In a little courtyard God's bright sun shone warm on the first day of spring. The sunbeams glided down the white wall of the neighbouring house. Close by grew the first yellow flower, shining like gold in the bright sunbeams. An old grandmother sat outdoors in her chair. Her pretty granddaughter, a poor serving girl home for a short visit, kissed her grandmother. There was gold, heart's gold, in that blessed kiss, gold on the lips, gold on the ground, gold in the morning hour.

"See, that is my little story," said the buttercup.

"Poor Grandmother!" sighed Gerda. "Yes, she is surely longing for me and grieving for me, just as she did for little Kay. But soon I shall go home again and bring Kay with me. There is no use in my asking the flowers: they only know their own song, and give me no information." Then she pulled up her skirt, so that she might run faster, but the jonquil struck her on the leg as she jumped over it, and she stopped to look at the tall flower.

"Do you, perhaps, know anything?" she asked.

She bent close down to the flower.

"I can see myself! I can see myself!" said the jonquil. "Oh! how sweet I smell! Up in the little attic stands a little dancing girl half dressed. She stands sometimes on one foot, sometimes on both; she seems to tread on the whole world. She's nothing but a delusion: she pours water out of a teapot on a bit of stuff—it is her bodice. 'Cleanliness is a good thing,' she says. Her white frock hangs on a hook; it has been washed in the teapot too, and dried on the roof. She puts it on and ties her saffron kerchief around her neck, and the dress looks even whiter. Point your toes! Look how she seems to stand on a stalk! I can see myself! I can see myself!"

"I don't care at all about that!" said Gerda. "It's no use your telling me!"

Then she ran to the end of the garden. The door was locked, but she pressed against the rusty latch. It gave way, the door sprang open, and little Gerda ran with bare feet out into the wide world. She looked back three times, but no one came after her. At last she could run no more, and she sat down on a big stone. When she looked around she saw that summer was over—it was already late autumn. No one could know that in the beautiful garden, where there was always sunshine, and where the flowers of every season were always blooming.

"Dear me, how much time I have lost," said Gerda. "It's already autumn! I mustn't stay any longer."

She got up to go. How sore and tired her feet were! Everything looked cold and bleak. The long willow leaves were yellow, and mist dripped from the trees like rain. One leaf dropped after another—only the wild plum still bore fruit, but the fruit was sour and set one's teeth on edge. Oh, how gray and gloomy it looked out in the wide world!

FOURTH STORY

The Prince and Princess

Soon Gerda had to rest again. Across the snow, just in front of where she was sitting, a big crow hopped. It stopped a long time to look at her, nodding its head, and then it said, "Caw! caw! Goo' day! Goo' day!" It couldn't say it any better, but it meant to be kind to the little girl, and asked where she was going all alone in the big wide world. Gerda understood the word *alone* very well, and felt how much it expressed. She told the crow the whole story of her life and fortunes, and asked if it had not seen her friend Kay.

And the crow nodded very gravely, and said:

"That may be! That may be!"

"You mean you've seen him?" cried the little girl, and nearly smothered the crow with kisses.

"Gently, gently!" said the crow. "I *think* I know: I believe it may be little Kay, but now he has certainly forgotten you for the Princess."

"Does he live with a Princess?" asked Gerda.

"Yes," said the crow. "Ah, it's so difficult for me to speak your language! If only you knew crows' language I could tell it much better."

"No, I never learned it," said Gerda, "but Grandmother understood it, and could speak it too. I only wish I had learned it."

"It doesn't matter," said the crow. "I will tell you as well as I can, but I'm afraid it will be rather badly."

Then the crow told her what it knew.

"In the country where we now are there lives a Princess who is quite wonderfully bright—but since she has read all the newspapers in the world and has forgotten them again, that probably explains it. Not long ago she was sitting on the throne—and that's not very much fun, they say—when she began to hum a song,

Why shouldn't I be married?

'Wait—there's something in that!' she said. And at once she felt she wanted to get married, but she wished for a husband who could answer when he was spoken to, not one who only stood and looked handsome, for that was a bore. So she called all her maids of honour together, and when they heard what she wanted they were delighted. 'You know what?' they said. 'I thought the same thing myself the other day.' You may be sure that every word I am telling you is true," said the crow. "I have a tame sweetheart who goes about freely in the castle, and she told me everything."

Of course, the sweetheart was a crow too, for birds of a feather flock together, and for a crow there is always another one.

"A notice was placed in the newspapers, with a border of hearts and the Princess's initials. It said that every young man who was good-looking might come to the castle and speak to the Princess, and the one who spoke in a way that showed he was most at home there, and who spoke best, would become the Princess's husband. Yes, yes," said the crow, "you can believe me. It's as true as I sit here. People came streaming in. There was a great to-do, much running to and fro, but no one succeeded either on the first or second day. They could all speak well enough when they were out in the streets, but when they entered the palace gates, and saw the guards in silver, and the lackeys in gold at the top of the staircase, and the great lighted halls, they became tongue-tied. When they stood in front of the throne where the Princess sat they could do nothing but repeat the last thing she had said, and, of course, she did not care to hear her own words again. It was as if the men in there had taken some sleeping powder and had fallen asleep until they got back into the street again, for not till then were they able to speak. There stood a whole row of them, from the town gate to the palace. I went out myself to see it," said the crow. "They were hungry and thirsty, but in the palace they did not receive so much as a glass of warm water. A few of the wisest had brought bread and butter with them, but they would not share with their neighbours, for they thought, 'Let him look hungry, and the Princess won't have him!' "

"But Kay, little Kay?" asked Gerda. "When did he come? Was he among the crowd?"

"Give me time! Give me time! We're just coming to him. It was on the third day that there came along a little person, without horse or carriage, walking quite merrily up to the castle. His eyes sparkled like yours, he had fine long hair, but his clothes were shabby."

"That was Kay!" cried Gerda, delighted. "Oh, then I have found him!" And she clapped her hands.

"He had a little knapsack on his back," said the crow.

"No, that must have been his sled," said Gerda, "for he went away with a sled."

"That may be," said the crow, "for I did not look very closely. But this much I know from my sweetheart, that when he came in through the palace gate and saw the guards in silver, and the lackeys in gold at the top of the staircase, he was not in the least self-conscious. He nodded and said to them, 'It must be tiresome standing on the stairs—I'd rather go in.' The halls were ablaze with lights; privy councillors and excellencies walked about with bare feet and carried golden vessels. It was enough to make anyone solemn! And his boots creaked dreadfully, but he was not at all frightened."

"That must have been Kay!" said Gerda. "I know he had new boots on; I've heard them creak in Grandmother's room."

"Yes, they certainly creaked," said the crow. "Anyway, he went boldly in to the Princess herself, who sat on a pearl as big as a spinning wheel. All the maids of honour with their maids and maids' maids, and all the cavaliers with their gentlemen followers and their gentlemen's gentlemen, who themselves had a page apiece, were standing around. And the nearer they stood to the door, the prouder they looked. The gentlemen's gentlemen's pages, who always wear slippers, could hardly be looked at, so proudly did they stand in the doorway!"

"That must be terrible!" said little Gerda. "And yet Kay won the Princess?"

"If I had not been a crow I would have taken her myself, although I am engaged. They say he spoke as well as I do when I speak crows' language, or so I heard from my sweetheart. He was witty and pleasant. He had not come to woo the Princess, but only to hear her wisdom, and he thought well of her, and she thought well of him."

"Yes, that must have been Kay!" said Gerda. "He was so clever, he could do arithmetic in his mind up to fractions. Oh, won't you take me to the palace too?"

"That's easily said," replied the crow. "But how are we to manage it? I'll talk it over with my tame sweetheart. She can probably advise us. But this I must tell you—a little girl like you will never get permission to go inside!"

"Oh, yes, I will," said Gerda. "When Kay hears that I'm there he'll come right out and fetch me."

"Wait for me over there at the stile," said the crow, and he wagged his head and flew away.

It was already late in the evening when the crow came back.

"Caw! caw!" he said. "I'm to greet you kindly from her, and give you this little loaf. She took it from the kitchen. There's bread enough there, and you must be hungry. You can't possibly get into the palace, for you are barefooted, and the guards in silver and the lackeys in gold wouldn't allow it. But don't cry; you'll get in somehow. My sweetheart knows a little back staircase that leads up to the bedroom, and she knows where she can get the key."

They went into the garden, into the great avenue, where the leaves were falling one after the other, and when the lights in the palace were put out one after the other, the crow led little Gerda to a back door that stood ajar.

Gerda's heart beat fast with fear and longing! She felt as if she were doing something wrong, and yet she only wanted to know if Kay was there. Yes, it must be he. She thought so earnestly of his bright eyes and his long hair; she could see how he smiled as he used to when they sat at home under the roses. He would surely be glad to see her, to hear what a long way she had come for his sake, and to know how sorry they had all been at home when he did not come back.

Now they were on the stairs. A little lamp was burning on a cupboard, and in the middle of the room stood the tame crow, turning her head from side to side and staring at Gerda, who curtsied as her grandmother had taught her.

"My betrothed has spoken to me very favourably of you, my little lady," said the tame crow. "Your story is really most touching. Will you take the lamp? I will go first. We will go straight along, for we shall meet nobody."

"I feel as if someone were coming after us," said Gerda, as she fancied something rushed by her. It seemed like shadows on the wall; horses with flowing manes and thin legs, hunters, and gentlemen and ladies on horseback.

"They are only dreams," said the crow. "They are coming to carry the nobles' thoughts out hunting. That's all the better, for you may look more closely at them in bed. But I hope, once you are taken into favour and are honoured, that you will show a grateful heart."

"Of that we may be sure!" said the crow from the wood.

They came to the first room: the walls were hung with rose-coloured satin embroidered with flowers. Here again the dreams came flitting by them, but they swept by so quickly that Gerda could not see the high-born lords and ladies. Each room was more splendid than the last. Then they came to the bedchamber. Here the ceiling was like a great palm tree with leaves of costly glass, and in the middle of the floor were two beds, each hung like a lily on a stalk of gold. One of them was white, and in that lay the Princess; the other was red, and in that it was that Gerda was to look for little Kay. She bent one of the red leaves aside and saw a brown neck. Yes indeed, it was Kay! She called his name and held the lamp over him. The dreams rushed on horseback through the room again—he awoke, turned his head, and—it was not little Kay!

The Prince was young and handsome, and the Princess peeped out, blinking, from the white lily bed, and asked what was the matter. Then little Gerda cried, and told them her whole story, and all that the crows had done for her.

"You poor little thing!" said the Prince and the Princess.

And they praised the crows and said that they were not angry with them at all, but they were not to do it again. However, they should be rewarded.

"Will you fly away free?" asked the Princess. "Or would you rather have permanent posts as Court crows?"

The two crows bowed and begged for permanent posts, for they thought of their old age, and said, "It is so good to have something put by for one's old age."

The Prince got up out of bed and let Gerda sleep in it, and he could not do more than that. She folded her little hands and thought, "How good men and animals are!" and then she shut her eyes and went quietly to sleep. All the dreams came flying by again, looking like God's angels, and they drew a little sled on which Kay sat and nodded. But it was only a dream, and so was gone again as soon as she awoke.

Next day she was dressed from head to toe in silk and velvet. She was invited to stay in the castle and enjoy herself, but instead she begged them to give her a little carriage and a horse and a pair of boots, so that she could drive out into the wide world again and find Kay.

They gave her both boots and a muff, and she was prettily dressed. When she was ready to leave, a new coach of pure gold was there for her before the door. On it was the coat of arms of the Prince and Princess, shining like a star. Coachman, footmen, and the postilions—for there were postilions too—all had golden crowns on their heads. The Prince and the Princess helped her into the carriage and wished her good luck. The forest crow, who was now married, accompanied her the first three miles. He sat by Gerda's side, for he could not bear to ride backwards. The other crow stood in the doorway, flapping her wings. She did not go with them for she had a bad headache: since she had gotten her permanent appointment, she had had too much to eat. The coach was stocked with sugar cakes, and under the seat there were ginger nuts and fruit.

"Farewell! Farewell!" cried the Prince and Princess, and little Gerda wept, and the crow wept. They went on like that for the first three miles, and then the crow said farewell too, and that was the saddest parting of all. Then he flew up into a tree, and beat his black wings as long as he could see the coach, which glittered like bright sunshine.

FIFTH STORY

The Little Robber Girl

They drove on through a dark forest, but the coach gleamed like a torch, which dazzled the robbers' eyes, and which they could not bear.

"Gold! Gold!" they cried, and rushed forward, seized the horses, killed the postilions, the coachman, and the footmen, and then dragged little Gerda out of the carriage.

"She is fat—she is pretty—she has been fattened on nuts!" said the old robber woman, who had a long matted beard and eyebrows that hung down over her eyes. "She's as good as a little fatted lamb! How good she will taste!"

She drew out her shining knife, which glittered in a horrible way.

"Oh!" screamed the old woman, for at the same moment her ear was bitten by her own little daughter, who hung on her back and was as wild and savage as an animal. "You ugly brat!" said her mother.

"I want her to play with me!" said the little robber girl. "I want her muff and her pretty dress, and I want her to sleep with me in my bed!"

Then she bit her mother again. The woman jumped high in the air and twisted and turned, and all the robbers laughed and said:

"Look how she dances with her young!"

"I want to ride in the carriage!" said the little robber girl.

And she got her own way, for she was spoiled and stubborn. She and Gerda sat in the carriage, and off they drove over stock and stone deep into the forest. The little robber girl was as big as Gerda, but stronger and more broad-shouldered, and she had dark skin. Her eyes were black and they looked almost sad. She took little Gerda around the waist and said:

"They won't kill you as long as I don't get angry with you. I suppose you are a princess?"

"No," replied Gerda. And she told her everything that had happened to her, and how fond she was of little Kay.

The robber girl looked at her earnestly, gave a little nod, and said:

"They won't kill you even if I *do* get angry with you, for then I will do it myself."

Then she dried Gerda's eyes, and put her two hands into the beautiful muff that was so soft and warm.

Soon the coach stopped, and they were in the courtyard of a robber's castle. Its walls had cracked from top to bottom; ravens and crows flew out of the open holes, and big bulldogs—each of which looked as if it could devour a man—jumped high in the air, but they did not bark, for that was forbidden.

In the great old smoky hall a big fire was burning in the middle of the stone floor. The smoke went up to the ceiling and had to find its own way out. A big cauldron of soup was boiling, and hares and rabbits were roasting on the spit.

"You shall sleep here tonight with me and all my animals," said the robber girl.

They got something to eat and drink, and then went over into a corner where some straw and some carpets were lying. Overhead, sitting on laths and perches, were nearly a hundred pigeons. They all seemed to be asleep, but they moved a little when the two girls arrived.

"They are all mine," said the little robber girl. She quickly seized one of those nearest, held it by the feet, and shook it till it flapped its wings. "Kiss it!" she cried, and beat it in Gerda's face. "There sit rascals from the wood," she went on, pointing to a number of laths that had been nailed in front of a hole high up in the wall. "Those are wood rascals, those two; they fly away at once if one does not keep them properly shut up. And here's my old sweetheart 'Bae.' " And she dragged out by the horns a reindeer that was tied up and had a polished copper ring around its neck. "We have to keep him tied up or he'd run away. Every evening I tickle his neck with my sharp knife, and that frightens him terribly!"

The little girl drew a long knife out of a crack in the wall and let it slide over the reindeer's neck. The poor animal kicked its legs. The robber girl only laughed and pulled Gerda into bed with her.

"Do you keep that knife with you while you sleep?" asked Gerda, and looked at it rather frightened.

"I always sleep with my knife," replied the robber girl. "One never knows what may happen. But tell me once again what you told me before about little Kay, and why you went out into the wide world."

So Gerda told it all over again, and the wood pigeons cooed above them in their cage, and the other pigeons slept. The little robber girl put her arm around Gerda's neck, held her knife in the other hand, and slept so that one could hear her. Gerda could not close her eyes at all, for she did not know whether she was going to live or die.

The robbers sat around the fire, sang, and drank, and the old robber woman turned somersaults. Gerda was even more terrified than before.

Then the wood pigeons said, "Coo! Coo! We have seen little Kay. A white hen was carrying his sled. He sat in the Snow Queen's carriage, which drove close by the forest as we lay in our nests. She blew upon us young pigeons, and all died except us two. Coo! Coo!"

"What are you saying up there?" asked Gerda. "Where was the Snow Queen going? Do you know anything about it?"

"She was probably going to Lapland, for there there's always ice and snow. Ask the reindeer."

"There indeed there is snow and ice," said the reindeer. "There one runs free in the wide glittering valleys! There the Snow Queen has her summer tent. But her stronghold is up nearer the North Pole, on the island they call Spitzbergen."

"Oh, Kay, poor little Kay!" sighed Gerda.

"You must lie still," said the robber girl, "or else you will feel the knife in your body."

In the morning Gerda told her all that the wood pigeons had said, and the robber girl looked very serious, nodded her head, and said to the reindeer:

"Do you know where Lapland is?"

"Of course I do!" said the animal, and its eyes shone. "I was born and bred there! There have I leaped about over the snowfields!"

"Listen!" said the robber girl to Gerda. "You see all the men have gone. Only Mother is still here, and she'll stay. But towards noon she drinks out of the big bottle, and then she falls asleep. Then I'll do something for you."

Then she sprang out of bed, and clasped her mother around the neck and pulled her beard, saying:

"Good morning, my own dear nanny goat!" And her mother banged her nose till it was all red. But it was all done out of pure love.

When the mother had drunk out of her bottle and was taking a little nap, the robber girl went to the reindeer and said:

"I would like very much to tickle you a few times more with this knife, for then you are so funny; but I won't. I'll loosen your rope and help you out, so that you may run away to Lapland. But you must use your legs well and carry this little girl to the palace of the Snow Queen, where her friend is. You've heard what she told me, for she spoke loud enough and you were listening."

The reindeer jumped with joy. The robber girl lifted Gerda up and gave her her own little cushion to sit on. "That's fine," she said, "and here are your fur boots too, for it's growing cold. But I will keep the muff for it's so pretty. Still, you won't freeze: here are my mother's big mittens—they'll reach right up to your elbows. Put them on! Now your hands look just like my ugly mother's!"

Gerda wept for joy.

"I can't bear to see you cry," said the little robber girl. "You ought to be delighted! And here are two loaves and a ham for you, so you won't starve."

She tied them on the reindeer's back. The little robber girl opened the door, called in all the big dogs, cut the rope with her knife, and said to the reindeer:

"Now run, but take good care of the little girl!"

Gerda stretched out her hands with the big mittens to the little robber girl, and cried "Good-bye!"

Off flew the reindeer, over stumps and stones, away through the great forest, over marshes and steppes, as fast as it could go. The wolves howled and the ravens croaked. "Hiss! Hiss!" it went in the air. It was as if the sky were red with fire.

"Those are my old Northern Lights," said the reindeer. "Look how they flash!" Then he ran on faster than ever, day and night.

They ate the loaves, and the ham too, and so at long last they reached Lapland.

SIXTH STORY

The Lapp Woman and the Finn Woman

They stopped at a little hut. It was a very humble hut. The roof sloped right down to the ground, and the door was so low that the family had to creep on their stomachs when they wanted to go in or out. No one was in the house but an old Lapp woman cooking fish over an oil lamp. The reindeer told her Gerda's history, but only after telling his own first, for that seemed more important. Gerda was so numbed with cold that she could not speak.

"Oh, you poor creatures!" said the Lapp woman. "You have a long way to run yet! You must go more than a hundred miles into Finmark, for the Snow Queen is there, staying in the country and burning blue lights every evening. I'll write a few words on a dried stockfish, for I have no paper, and I'll give you that to take to the Finn woman up there. She can give you better information than I."

When Gerda was warmer, and had had something to eat and drink, the Lapp woman wrote a few words on a dried stockfish, bid Gerda to take good care of it, put her on the reindeer again, and away they went. Flash! Flash! It went up in the sky. All night long the beautiful blue Northern Lights burned.

When they got to Finmark, they knocked at the chimney of the Finn woman, for she had no door at all.

It was so hot inside that the Finn woman herself went about

almost naked. She was very small and very grimy. She hastened to loosen Gerda's things and take off her mittens and boots, for otherwise it would have been too hot for her. Next she laid a piece of ice on the reindeer's head, and read what was written on the stockfish. She read it three times, and when she knew it by heart, she put the fish into the kettle, for it was good to eat, and she never wasted anything.

Then the reindeer told his own story first, and little Gerda's after, and the Finn woman blinked her wise eyes, but said nothing.

"You are so clever," said the reindeer. "I know you can tie all the winds of the world together with a bit of thread; if the skipper undoes one knot he has a good wind; if he undoes the second it blows hard; but if he undoes the third and the fourth there is such a tempest that the forests are blown down. Won't you give this little girl a draught, so that she may get twelve men's strength and overcome the Snow Queen?"

"Twelve men's strength!" said the Finn woman. "Much good that would be!"

And she went to a shelf and took down a great rolled-up skin and unrolled it. Strange characters were written upon it, and the Finn woman read until water ran down her forehead.

But the reindeer begged again so hard for little Gerda, and Gerda looked at the Finn woman with beseeching eyes so full of tears that the woman began to blink back her own tears. She drew the reindeer into a corner and whispered to him, while she laid fresh ice upon his head:

"Little Kay is certainly at the Snow Queen's, and finds everything there to his taste and liking. In fact, he thinks it's the best place in the world, but that is because he has a splinter of glass in his eye and a grain of glass in his heart. These must be removed, or he will never be human again, and the Snow Queen will keep her power over him."

"Can't you give Gerda something that will help her?"

"I can give her no greater power than she already has. Don't you see how great that is? Don't you see how man and beast are obliged to serve her, and how with her bare feet she has got on so well in the world? She must not be told of her power. It is in her heart, and there it will remain, because she is such a dear innocent child. If she herself cannot reach the Snow Queen and remove the bits of glass from little Kay, we can be of no help! Two miles from here the Snow Queen's garden begins. You can take Gerda there. Set her down by the big bush with the red berries that stands in the snow. Don't stop there gossiping, but hurry back here again!"

Saying that, the Finn woman lifted little Gerda onto the reindeer, which ran off as fast as he could.

"Oh, I have left my boots! And my mittens!" cried Gerda, as soon as she felt the biting cold. But the reindeer did not stop: he ran on till he came to the bush with the red berries. There he put Gerda down and kissed her on the mouth. Big bright tears ran down the creature's cheeks; and then it ran back, as fast as it could. There stood poor Gerda without shoes, without gloves, in the midst of the terrible icy Finmark.

She ran on as fast as she could. She was met by a whole regiment of snowflakes, which were not falling from the sky, for that was quite bright and shone with the Northern Lights. No, the snowflakes ran along the ground, and the nearer they came the larger they grew. Gerda still remembered how large and curious the snow-flakes had appeared when she looked at them through the magnifying glass. But here they were far larger and much more terrible—in fact, they were alive! They were the Snow Queen's advance guard and they had the strangest shapes. Some looked like big ugly porcupines, others like knots of snakes stretching out their heads; others were like little fat bears whose hair stood on end. All were dazzling white; all were living snowflakes.

Then little Gerda said a prayer. The cold was so great that she could see her own breath, which came out of her mouth like smoke. Her breath became thicker and thicker and formed itself into bright little angels, who grew and grew as soon as they touched the earth. All had helmets on their heads and shields and spears in their hands. Their numbers kept increasing, and when Gerda had finished her prayer, a whole legion stood around her. They thrust their spears at the terrible snowflakes, so that these were shattered into a hundred pieces. Little Gerda could now go safely on her way. The angels rubbed her hands and feet, so that she did not feel the cold so much, and she hurried on to the Snow Queen's palace.

Now we will see what Kay is doing. He certainly is not thinking of little Gerda, nor does he have any inkling that she is standing in front of the palace.

SEVENTH STORY

*Of the Snow Queen's Castle and What
Happened There at Last*

The walls of the palace were made of the drifting snow, the windows and doors of the cutting winds. There were more than a hundred halls, all formed by the drifting snow. The largest of them extended for several miles; they were all lit up by the strong Northern Lights, and how wide and empty, how icy cold and glittering they all were! There never was any merriment there, not even a little bears' ball, at which the storm could have played the music, while the polar bears walked about on their hind legs and showed off their pretty manners; never any parlour games, or any little tea parties among the young lady arctic foxes. Empty, vast, and cold were the halls of the Snow Queen. The Northern Lights flamed so brightly that they could be counted both when they were highest in the sky and when they were lowest. In the middle of this empty endless snow hall was a frozen lake. It had cracked into a thousand pieces, but each piece was so exactly like the rest that it was a perfect work of art. In the middle of the lake sat the Snow Queen when she was at home. She was fond of saying that she sat in the mirror of understanding, and that this was the only one, and the best in the world.

Little Kay was blue with cold—indeed, nearly black. He did not feel it, though, for she had kissed away his icy shiverings, and his heart was like a lump of ice. He was dragging some sharp flat pieces of ice to and fro, joining them together in all kinds of ways, for he wanted to make something out of them. It was just like a Chinese puzzle. Kay was making patterns too—and very artistic ones. It was the ice game of reason. In his eyes the patterns were very remarkable and of the highest importance; that was because of the speck of glass in his eye. He laid out whole patterns, so that they formed words—but he could never manage to make the word he wanted—the word *eternity*.

The Snow Queen had said: "If you can make that word you shall be your own master, and I will give you the whole world and a new pair of skates."

But try as he might he could not.

"Now I must fly away to warm countries," said the Snow Queen. "I will go and peep into the black cauldrons." She meant the burning volcanoes, Etna and Vesuvius, as they are called. "I'll whiten them a little. It will be good for the lemons and the grapes."

So away flew the Snow Queen, and Kay sat all alone in the great empty mile-long ice hall and gazed at his pieces of ice, and thought and thought till cracks were heard inside him: one would have thought that he was frozen.

It was then that little Gerda entered the castle by the great gate. Here cutting winds kept guard, but she said the evening prayer, and the winds dropped as if they wanted to go to sleep. She went deeper and deeper into the great icy halls, until she finally saw Kay. She recognized him and flew to him. She embraced him and held him fast, and called out:

"Kay, dear little Kay! At long last I have found you!"

But he sat quite still, stiff and cold. Then little Gerda wept hot tears, which fell upon his breast. They penetrated into his heart;

they thawed the lump of ice and melted the little piece of glass in it. He looked at her, and she sang the hymn:

> Roses fade and die, but we
> Our Infant Lord shall surely see.

Then Kay burst into tears. He wept so that the splinter of glass was washed out of his eye. And then he knew her, and cried joyfully: "Gerda, dear little Gerda! Where have you been all this time? And where have I been?" And he looked around him. "How cold it is here! How empty and vast!"

He held fast to Gerda, and she laughed and wept for joy. Such was their joy that even the pieces of ice danced about them. And when they were tired and lay down again, the shards of ice formed themselves into the very letters the Snow Queen meant when she said that if he found them out he should be his own master, and she would give him the whole world and a new pair of skates.

Gerda kissed Kay's cheeks, and they turned pink. She kissed his eyes, and they shone like her own. She kissed his hands and feet, and he became well and merry. The Snow Queen might come home now; there stood his discharge, written in shining blocks of ice.

They took each other by the hand and went out of the great palace. They talked of the grandmother, and of the roses on the roof, and wherever they went the winds sank to rest and the sun came out. When they came to the bush with the red berries, the reindeer was standing there waiting. He had brought with him another young reindeer, whose udder was full, and who gave the children warm milk and kissed them on the mouth. Then they carried

Kay and Gerda, first to the Finn woman, where they warmed themselves in the hot room and received instructions for their journey home, and then to the Lapp woman, who had made clothes for them and got their sled ready for them.

The reindeer and the young one ran free by their side, and followed them to the frontier of the country, where the first green leaves were budding. There they took leave of the two reindeer and the Lapp woman. "Farewell!" they all said. And once more they heard the birds twitter and saw the forest all decked with green buds, and out of it, on a splendid horse which Gerda knew, for it had drawn her golden coach, a young girl came riding, with a bright red cap on her head and pistols in her belt. It was the little robber girl, who had grown tired of staying at home and wished first to go north and, if she didn't like that, then somewhere else. She knew Gerda at once, and Gerda knew her too; it was a joyful meeting.

"A fine fellow you are running off like that," she said to Kay. "I don't think you deserve this lovely creature, who's gone looking for you to the end of the earth."

But Gerda patted her cheeks and asked about the Prince and Princess.

"They've gone to foreign countries," said the robber girl.

"But the crow?" said Gerda.

"Why, the crow is dead," answered the other. "The tame sweetheart is a widow and goes about with a bit of black worsted around her leg. She complains most sadly, but it's all talk. But now tell me about your journey, and how you finally found him."

So Gerda and Kay told their story.

"My, what an exciting tale!" said the robber girl.

And she took them both by the hand and promised that if she ever came through their town she would pay them a visit. And then she rode away into the wide world. Gerda and Kay went on hand in hand, and as they went the spring became lovely with flowers and verdure. The church bells rang, and they recognized the high steeples and the great town in which they lived. On they went to the grandmother's door, and up the stairs, and into the room, where everything stood in the same place as before. The big clock was going "Tick! Tick!" and the hands moved; but as they went in through the door they noticed that they had become grown-up people. The roses out on the roof gutter were blooming at the open window, and there stood their little children's stools. Kay and Gerda sat down on their own stools, and held each other by the hand. They had forgotten the cold empty grandeur of the Snow Queen's castle as if it were a heavy dream. Grandmother was sitting in God's bright sunshine, and she read aloud from the Bible, "Except ye become as little children, ye shall in no wise enter into the kingdom of God."

And Kay and Gerda looked into each other's eyes, and all at once they understood the old hymn:

> Roses fade and die, but we
> Our Infant Lord shall surely see.

There they both sat, grown-up and yet children—children at heart—and it was summer, warm lovely summer.

❧ The Wild Swans ❧

FAR AWAY, where the swallows fly when winter comes, there lived a King who had eleven sons, and one daughter, Eliza. The eleven brothers were all Princes, and each one went to school with a star on his breast and his sword by his side. They wrote with diamond pencils on slates of gold and learned by heart just as easily as they read: one could see immediately that they were Princes. Their sister, Eliza, sat on a little stool made of plate glass and had a picture book that was worth at least half a kingdom.

The children were very happy, but their happiness was not to last forever.

Their father, who was King of the whole country, married a wicked Queen who did not love her stepchildren at all. It did not take them long to find this out. There was a party at the palace with lots of guests. The children were playing games, pretending to receive the guests, but instead of being given all the spare cake and all the roasted apples they wanted, they were only given some sand in a teacup, and were told that they should make believe it was really good.

The following week the Queen sent Eliza to the country to stay with a peasant and his wife. She told the King so many lies about the Princes that he decided it would be a waste of time to think about them anymore.

"Fly out into the world and make your own way," said the wicked Queen. "Fly like great birds without a voice."

But she could not make it as bad for them as she wanted, for the Princes turned into eleven magnificent wild swans. With a strange cry, they flew out of the palace windows, over the park, and into the woods.

It was still early morning when they flew over the place where their sister, Eliza, lay in the peasant's cottage. They hovered over the roof, craned their long necks and flapped their wings, but no one heard or saw them. They were obliged to fly on, up towards the clouds, far away into the wide world. Then they flew on to a great dark woods, which stretched all the way to the seashore.

Poor little Eliza stood in the peasant's cottage and played with a green leaf, for she had no toys. She pricked a hole in the leaf and looked through it up at the sun. It seemed to her as if she had seen her brothers' bright eyes. Each time the warm sun shone on her cheeks, she thought of all the kisses they had given her.

One day passed just like another. When the wind swept through the rose bushes next to the house, it seemed to whisper to them: "What can be more beautiful than you?" But the rose bushes shook their heads and answered, "Eliza!" When the old woman sat in front of her door on Sunday and read in her prayer book, the wind turned the pages and said to the book, "Who can be more pious than you?" and the book said, "Eliza!" And what the rose bushes and the prayer book said was simply the truth.

When she was fifteen, Eliza went home. When the Queen saw how beautiful she was, she was furious and full of hatred. She wished she could change her into a wild swan too, but she didn't

dare, at least not right away, because the King wanted to see his daughter.

Early in the morning of Eliza's return, the Queen went into her bathroom, which was built of white marble and filled with soft cushions and the most beautiful rugs. She took three toads, kissed them, and said to the first:

"Sit on Eliza's head when she comes into the bath, so that she may become as stupid as you."

"Sit on her forehead," she said to the second, "so that she may become as ugly as you, and her father won't recognize her."

"Lie on her heart," she whispered to the third, "so that she may have an evil temper and suffer from it."

Then she put the toads into the clear water, which at once turned green. She called Eliza and told her to undress and step into the water. When Eliza stepped into her bath, one of the toads sat on her hair, the second on her forehead, and the third on her heart, but Eliza did not seem to notice them. When she rose, three red poppies were floating on the water. If the creatures had not been poisonous, and if the witch had not kissed them, they would have been changed into red roses. They became flowers because they had rested on the girl's head and forehead and heart. She was too good and innocent for the Queen's sorcery to have any power over her.

When the wicked Queen saw what had happened, she rubbed Eliza with walnut juice, so that she became dark brown, and smeared ointment on her face, and let her beautiful hair hang in wild disarray. By the time she was finished, it was impossible to recognize Eliza.

When her father saw her he was terribly shocked, and declared that this girl was not his daughter. No one but the dog and the swallows recognized her, but they were only poor animals who counted for nothing.

Then Eliza wept and thought of her eleven lost brothers. She crept out of the castle, and walked all day over the fields and meadows till she came to the big forest. She didn't know where to go. She felt very sad and longed for her brothers; she was sure something terrible had happened to them, too, although she didn't know quite what. All she knew was that she must try to find them.

She had been in the woods only a short time when night fell. She lost the path, and so she lay down on the soft moss, said her prayers, and laid her head against the stump of a tree. The woods were quiet, the air was mild, and in the grass and in the moss hundreds of glowworms gleamed like tiny dots of green fire. When she touched one of the branches with her hand, the shining insects showered down on her like shooting stars.

All night long she dreamed of her brothers. They were children again, playing together, writing with their diamond pencils on their golden slates, and looking at the beautiful picture book that had cost half a kingdom. But now they were not writing lines and letters as they had once done, but were telling the brave deeds they had performed, and all they had seen and experienced. What was more, in the picture book everything was alive—the birds sang, and the people stepped out of the book and spoke with Eliza and her brothers. But when the page was turned, they jumped back in again, so that the people on the next page could have their proper turn.

When she awoke the sun was already high in the sky. She could not see it, though, for the trees spread their lofty branches far and wide above her. But the sunbeams shimmered there above like a gauzy veil, there was the fresh smell of grass, and the birds flew so close they almost perched on her shoulders. She could hear the splashing of water from a number of springs, all of which flowed into a lake that had the softest sandy bottom. It was surrounded by thick bushes, except at one point where the stags had made a large opening, and here Eliza went down to the water. The lake was so clear that if the wind had not stirred the branches and the bushes, one would have thought they were painted on the bottom of the lake, so clearly was every leaf mirrored, whether bathed in sunlight or steeped in shadow.

When Eliza saw her own face—stained so brown—she was terrified; but when she wet her hand and rubbed her eyes and her forehead, the white skin shone through again. Then she undressed and went into the fresh water: a more beautiful Princess than she could not be found in the whole world.

When she had dressed again and plaited her long hair, she went to the rippling spring, drank out of the hollow of her hand, and then wandered deeper into the woods, not knowing where she was going. She thought of her brothers, and of God, who would certainly not forsake her. It is He who lets the wild apples grow, to satisfy the hungry. He showed her a crab apple tree, with its boughs bending under the weight of the fruit. Here she ate her noon meal. She put props under the boughs, and then went on into the darkest part of the forest. It was so still that she could hear the sound of her own footsteps and the rustling of every dry leaf underfoot. Not a bird was to be seen, not a ray of sunlight found its way through the great dark branches of the trees. The lofty trunks stood so close together that when she looked around it appeared as though a stout fence was hemming her in on every side. She was lonelier than she had ever been before!

The night grew very dark. Not a single glowworm gleamed in the marsh. Sadly she lay down to sleep. Then it seemed to her as if the branches above her head parted, and the mild eyes of Jesus Himself looked down on her, with tiny angels peeping out from behind his head and arms.

When morning came she did not know if it had really happened, or if she had dreamed it.

She went a little farther and met an old woman with a basket full of berries, and the old woman gave her a few to eat. Eliza asked her if she had seen eleven Princes riding through the forest.

"No," replied the old woman, "but yesterday I saw eleven swans, with golden crowns on their heads, swimming in the river close by."

And she led Eliza a short distance to a slope, at the foot of which a stream wound its way. The trees on its bank stretched their long leafy branches across the stream towards each other, and where their natural growth did not allow them to come together, they had wrenched their roots from the ground until they were able to bend out over the water and let their branches twine together.

Eliza said good-bye to the old woman, and followed the river to where the stream flowed out to the great open sea.

The whole glorious expanse of sea lay before the young girl's eyes, but not one sail appeared, not a boat was to be seen. How could she go any farther? She looked at the countless pebbles on the shore; the water had worn them smooth. Glass, ironstones, everything there had been shaped by the water, which was much softer than even her delicate hand.

"The water rolls on endlessly, and what is hard becomes smooth. I will be just as unwearied. Thanks for your lesson, you clear rolling waves. My heart tells me that one day you will lead me to my beloved brothers."

On the foam-covered seaweed lay eleven white swan feathers, which she gathered into a bunch. There were drops of water on them—whether they were dewdrops or tears nobody could tell. It was lonely there on the beach, but she did not feel it, for the sea constantly changed—more in a few hours than the lovely lakes do in a whole year. When a great black cloud came over, it was as if the sea wanted to say "I can look angry too." And when the wind blew, the waves showed their white caps. But if the clouds gleamed red and the winds rested, the sea looked like a rose leaf, sometimes green, sometimes white. But however quiet it might be, there was always a slight motion by the shore: the water rose and fell gently, like the breast of a sleeping child.

When the sun was just about to set, Eliza saw eleven wild swans, with crowns on their heads, flying towards land. They flew in single file, so that they looked like a long white ribbon. Then Eliza climbed up the slope and hid behind a bush. The swans alighted near her and flapped their great white wings.

As soon as the sun had disappeared beneath the horizon, the swans' feathers fell off, and eleven handsome Princes—Eliza's brothers—stood before her! She uttered a loud cry, for although they were much changed, she felt it must be they. And so she sprang into their arms and called them by name. The Princes were surprised and happy to see their little sister again, and they recognized her, although she was now tall and beautiful. They laughed and cried; and now they fully understood how cruel their stepmother had been to them all.

"We brothers," said the eldest, "fly about as wild swans as long as the sun is up, but as soon as it sets we recover our human form. Therefore, we must always make sure that we have a resting place for our feet when the sun sets, for if at that moment we were flying up among the clouds, we would plunge down into the depths of the sea. We don't live here: there is a land just as beautiful as this beyond the sea, but the way there is long. We must cross the mighty sea, and along our way there is no island where we could spend the night, only a little rock halfway across. It is just large enough for us to stand on, close together. If the sea is rough, the waves splash over us, but we thank God for it. There we pass the night in still human form. Were it not for this rock, we could never visit our beloved homeland, for it takes two of the longest days in the year for our journey. Only once every year are we allowed to visit our home. For eleven days we can stay there and fly over the big forest, from where we can see the palace in which we were born and in which our father lives, and the high church tower, in whose shadow our mother lies buried. Here the bushes and trees seem familiar to us; the wild horses race across the plains, as we saw them do in our childhood; here the charcoal burner still sings the same old songs we danced to as children. This is our fatherland. We feel ourselves drawn to it, and here we have found you, dear little sister. We may stay here two days more, but then we must fly back across the sea to a land, which, however lovely, is not our own. How can we take you with us? We have neither ship nor boat."

"And how can I deliver you?" asked their sister; and they talked most of the night, only sleeping for a few hours.

Eliza was awakened by the rustling of the swans' wings above her. Her brothers were again transformed, and they flew in wide circles until at last they were far away. But one of them, the youngest, remained behind, and laid his swan's head in her lap, while she stroked his wings. They remained together all day. Towards evening the others came back, and when the sun had gone down they stood there in their own shapes.

"Tomorrow we must fly far away from here, and we cannot come back for a whole year. But we cannot leave you here! Have you the courage to come with us? My arm is strong enough to carry you through the woods; shouldn't all our wings be strong enough to fly with you over the sea?"

"Yes, take me with you," said Eliza.

They spent the whole night weaving a net of the pliant willow bark and tough reeds. It was both big and strong. Eliza lay down on it. When the sun rose and her brothers were changed back into wild swans, they seized the net with their beaks and flew with their beloved sister, who was still asleep, high up among the clouds. The sunbeams fell directly on her face, so one of the swans flew above her so that his broad wings might keep her face in shadow.

They were far away from the shore when Eliza awoke: she thought she was still dreaming, so strange did it seem to be carried high through the air over the sea. By her side lay a branch with beautiful ripe berries and a bundle of sweet roots, which her youngest brother had collected for her. She smiled at him gratefully, for she recognized him: it was he who was flying over her and shading her with his wings.

They were so high that the first ship they saw beneath them seemed like a white seagull floating on the water. A great cloud rose behind them, like a mountain, and on it Eliza saw her own shadow and those of the eleven swans, looking gigantic in size. It was a more beautiful picture than she had ever seen before. But as the sun rose higher, the cloud fell farther behind, and the floating shadow soon vanished.

On they flew all day long, like whizzing arms, but their flight was slower than usual for they had their sister to carry. A storm came up as the evening drew near. Eliza looked anxiously at the setting sun, for the lonely rock in the ocean could still not be seen. It seemed to her as if the swans were beating their wings more strongly. Alas! she was the cause of their not being able to fly any faster. When the sun went down, they would become men again and fall into the sea and drown. Then she prayed as hard as she could, but still she could see no rock. Dark clouds approached in a great black threatening body, rolling forwards like a mass of lead, and the lightning burst forth, flash after flash.

Now the sun touched the rim of the horizon. Eliza's heart trembled. Suddenly the swans plunged downwards, so swiftly that she thought they were falling, but they paused again. The sun was half hidden below the water, when for the first time she saw the little rock beneath her, and it looked no larger than a seal, thrusting its head above water. The sun sank very fast, until it appeared no larger than a star, and then her foot touched solid land. The sun was extinguished like the last spark in a piece of burned paper.

Her brothers were standing around her arm in arm, but there was barely enough room for all of them. The waves beat against the rock and showered them like rain. The sky glowed with constantly flashing lightning, and peal on peal of thunder rolled, but sister and brothers held each other by the hand and sang hymns, which gave them comfort and courage.

At dawn the air was pure and calm. As soon as the sun rose the swans flew with Eliza away from the tiny island. The sea still ran high, and when they soared aloft, the white foam looked like millions of white swans floating on the water.

When the sun rose higher, Eliza saw before her, half floating in the air, a mountain range capped with shining masses of ice. In the midst of it rose a castle a mile long, with row on row of elegant columns. Down below palm trees waved and there were bright flowers as large as millwheels. She asked if this was the country to which they were going, but the swans shook their heads, for what she saw was the beautiful, ever-changing palace of Fata Morgana, into which no mortal could enter. As Eliza gazed at it, the mountains, woods, and castle vanished, and in their place stood twenty proud churches, all nearly alike, with high towers and pointed windows. She imagined she could hear the organs playing, but it was only the sea. When she drew near the churches, they changed into a fleet sailing beneath her, but when she looked down it was only a sea mist drifting over the ocean.

It was an ever-changing scene that unfolded before her eyes, until at last she saw the real land to which they were bound. There arose the most glorious blue mountains, with cedar forests, cities, and palaces. Long before the sun went down she sat on a rock in front of a great cave overgrown with delicate green trailing plants like embroidered tapestry.

"Now we shall see what you will dream of here tonight," said the youngest brother, and he showed her to her bedroom.

"If only I could dream of how to save you," she said.

This thought possessed her so strongly, and she prayed so hard for help, even in her sleep she continued to pray. Then it seemed to her as if she were flying high through the air to Fata Morgana's palace, and the fairy came out to meet her, beautiful and radiant, and yet strikingly like the old woman who had given her the berries in the woods and had told her of the swans with golden crowns on their heads.

"Your brothers can be saved," she said. "But do you have the courage and perseverance? True, water is softer than your delicate hands, and yet it changes the shape of the stones. But it feels no pain as your fingers will; it has no heart, and cannot suffer the agony and torment you will have to endure. Do you see this stinging nettle I hold in my hand? Many of the same kind grow around the cave in which you sleep: only those, and the ones that grow on churchyard graves, are of use to you, remember that. These you must pick, though they will burn and blister your hands. Crush these nettles to pieces with your feet, and you will have a kind of flax. With this you must plait and weave eleven shirts of mail with long sleeves: throw these over the eleven swans, and the spell will be broken. But remember, from the moment you begin this work until it is finished, even if it should take years to finish, you must not speak. The first word you utter will pierce your brothers' hearts like a deadly dagger. Their lives hang on your tongue. Remember this well!"

She touched her hand with the nettle; it was like a burning fire and woke Eliza up.

It was already broad daylight; and close by where she had been sleeping lay a nettle like the one she had seen in her dream. She fell on her knees and gave thanks; then went from the cave to begin her work.

With her delicate hands she picked the ugly nettles. They stung like fire, raising big blisters on her arms and hands, but she felt she could bear it gladly if only she could free her dear brothers. Then she crushed every nettle with her bare feet and plaited the green flax.

When the sun set her brothers came, and they were frightened when they found she couldn't talk. They thought it was some new spell from their wicked stepmother, but when they saw her hands they understood what she was doing for their sake. The youngest brother wept, and where his tears fell she felt no more pain, and the burning blisters vanished.

She worked all night, for she could not sleep until she had delivered her dear brothers. All the next day, while the swans were away, she sat in solitude, but never had time flown so quickly. One shirt of mail was already finished, and she began the second.

Then a hunting horn sounded among the mountains, and she was frightened. The noise came nearer and nearer. She heard the barking of dogs. She fled into the cave, gathered the nettles she had collected into a bundle, and sat down.

Suddenly a big dog came bounding out of the woods, and then another, and another. They barked loudly, ran back, and then came again. A few minutes later all the huntsmen stood before the cave, and the handsomest of them was the King of the country. He came towards Eliza, for he had never seen a more beautiful maiden.

"How did you come here, my pretty child?" he asked.

Eliza shook her head, for she dared not speak—it would cost her brothers their deliverance and their lives. And she hid her hands under her apron, so that the King might not see what she was suffering.

"Come with me," he said. "You cannot stay here. If you are as good as you are beautiful, I will dress you in velvet and silk and place the golden crown on your head, and you shall live with me in my richest castle and rule."

And then he lifted her on his horse. She wept and wrung her hands, but the King said:

"I only want your happiness. One day you will thank me for this."

And then he galloped away into the mountains with her on his horse, and the hunters galloped behind.

When the sun went down, the royal city lay before them, with its churches and cupolas; and the King led her into the castle, where great fountains played in the lofty marble halls, and where the walls and ceilings were covered with beautiful paintings. But she had no eyes for all this—she only wept and mourned. Passively she let the women dress her in royal robes, weave pearls in her hair, and draw dainty gloves over her blistered fingers.

When she stood there in full array, she was dazzlingly beautiful,

so that the Court bowed deeper than ever. And the King chose her for his bride, although the archbishop shook his head and whispered that the beautiful maid must certainly be a witch, who had blinded the eyes and ensnared the heart of the King.

But the King ordered that music should be played, the costliest dishes should be served, and the most beautiful maidens should dance before them. She was led through fragrant gardens into gorgeous halls; but never a smile came upon her lips or shone in her eyes: she stood there, a picture of eternal grief.

Then the King opened the door of a little chamber close by where she was to sleep. This room was adorned with a lovely green tapestry and resembled exactly the cave where she had been found. On the floor lay the bundle of flax that she had prepared from the nettles, and from the ceiling hung the shirt of mail she had completed. One of the huntsmen had brought all these things with him as curiosities.

"Here you may dream that you are back in your former home," said the King. "Here is the work which occupied you there, and now, in the midst of all your splendour, it may amuse you to think of that time."

When Eliza saw these things that were so near her heart, a smile played around her mouth and the blood came back into her cheeks. She thought of her brothers' deliverance, and kissed the King's hand; he pressed her to his heart and ordered all the church bells to ring, announcing their forthcoming wedding feast. The beautiful dumb girl from the woods was to become the Queen of the country.

Then the archbishop whispered evil words into the King's ear, but they did not sink into the King's heart. The wedding was to take place; the archbishop himself had to place the crown on her head. In his anger, he pressed the narrow circlet so tightly on her forehead that it pained her. But a heavier weight lay on her heart— sorrow for her brothers. She did not feel any bodily pain. Her mouth was dumb, for a single word would cost her brothers their lives, but her eyes glowed with love for the kind, handsome King, who did everything to make her happy. She loved him with her whole heart, more and more every day. Oh how she wished that she had been able to confide in him and to tell him of her grief! But no, she had to remain dumb, and finish her work in silence. There- fore, at night, she crept away from his side, and went quietly into the little chamber that was decorated like the cave, and wove one shirt of mail after another. But when she began the seventh she had no flax left.

She knew that in the churchyard some nettles were growing that she could use. But she had to pluck them herself, and how was she to get there?

"Alas! What is the pain in my fingers compared to the torment in my heart?" she thought. "I must at least try. Surely Heaven will not deny me!"

With a trembling heart, as if she were doing something evil, she crept into the garden one moonlit night and stole through the lanes and the deserted streets to the churchyard. There, on one of the broadest tombstones, she saw a circle of ugly creatures. These hid- eous witches took off their ragged garments, as if they were going to bathe. Then with their long, skinny fingers they clawed open the fresh graves, and with fiendish greed they snatched the corpses and devoured the flesh. Eliza was obliged to pass close by them, and they fastened their evil glances on her. But she prayed silently, collected the burning nettles, and carried them back to the castle.

Only one person had seen her, the archbishop, for he stayed awake while the others slept. Now he felt sure he was right: she *was* a witch, and had bewitched not only the King but the whole people.

In the confessional he told the King what he had seen and what he feared. When those harsh words came from his tongue, the pictures of the saints in the cathedral shook their heads, as if to say: "It is not true! Eliza is innocent!" But the archbishop interpreted this differently. He thought they were bearing witness against her and shaking their heads at her sinfulness.

Two big tears rolled down the King's cheeks. He went home with doubt in his heart. At night he pretended to be asleep, but sleep did not come, for he noticed that Eliza got up every night. Each time he followed her silently and saw how she disappeared into her chamber.

Day by day his face became darker. Eliza saw it, but did not understand why. But it frightened her—and what anguish did she not suffer in her heart for her brothers? Her salt tears flowed upon the royal velvet and purple; they lay there like sparkling diamonds, and all who saw their splendour wished they were Queens.

In the meantime she had almost finished her work. Only one shirt of mail was still unfinished, but she had no flax left and not a single nettle. One last time, therefore, she would have to go to the churchyard to pick a few handfuls. She thought with terror of this solitary walk and of the horrible creatures there, but her will was as firm as her trust in Providence.

Eliza went, but the King and the archbishop followed her. They saw her go into the churchyard through the wicket gate. When they drew near, the ugly creatures were sitting on the gravestones, just as Eliza had seen them. The King turned aside, for he imagined that she, whose head had rested against his breast that very evening, must be one of them.

"The people must judge her," he said.

And the people did, and condemned her to death by fire.

She was taken from the magnificent royal palace into a dark damp cell, where the wind whistled through the grated window. Instead of velvet and silk they gave her the bundle of nettles she had collected: on this she could lay her head. And the hard burning coats of mail that she had woven were to be her coverlet. But nothing could have been given her that she liked better. She resumed her work and prayed. Outside, the street boys were singing jeering songs about her, and not a soul comforted her.

Towards evening there came the whirring of swans' wings close by the prison window—it was the youngest of her brothers. He had found his sister, and she sobbed aloud with joy, though she knew that the approaching night would probably be her last. But now the work was almost finished and her brothers were near.

The archbishop came to stay with her during her last hours, for he had promised the King he would. But she shook her head, and with looks and gestures begged him to leave, for that night she had to finish her work, or else all would be in vain—all her tears, her pain, and her sleepless nights. The archbishop withdrew, uttering bitter words against her, but poor Eliza knew she was innocent, and continued her work.

The little mice ran back and forth, dragging the nettles to her feet, to help her as best they could, while outside the grating of the cell window a thrush sang the whole night through, to help her keep up her courage.

It was still not dawn. In an hour the sun would rise. The eleven brothers stood at the castle gate and demanded to be brought before the King. That could not be, they were told, for it was still night. The King was asleep and could not be disturbed. They begged, they threatened, and the sentries came, yes, finally even the King himself came out, and he asked what was the meaning of this. At that very moment the sun rose, and the brothers were no longer to be seen. But over the castle eleven wild swans flew.

All the people came flocking out through the town gate, for they wanted to see the witch burned. A wretched old horse drew the cart on which she sat. They had dressed her in a garment of coarse sackcloth. Her lovely hair hung loose about her beautiful head. Her cheeks were deathly pale, and her lips moved silently, while her fingers were still busy weaving the green flax. Even on her way to death she did not interrupt the work she had begun. The ten shirts of mail lay at her feet, and she worked on the eleventh. The mob jeered at her.

"Look at the witch, how she mutters! She has no hymn book in her hand. No, there she sits with her ugly sorcery. Tear it away from her and into a thousand pieces!"

And they all surged around her, wanting to tear up the shirts of mail. Then eleven wild swans swooped down and sat around her on the cart, flapping their wings. The terrified mob gave way before them.

"It is a sign from heaven! She is certainly innocent!" whispered many. But they did not dare say it aloud.

Now the executioner seized her by the hand, but she hastily threw the eleven shirts over the swans, and immediately eleven handsome Princes stood before them. But the youngest had a swan's wing instead of an arm, for one of his shirtsleeves was missing—she had not quite finished it.

"Now I may speak!" she said. "I am innocent!"

And the people who saw what happened bowed before her as before a saint, but she sank lifelessly into her brothers' arms, for the suspense, anguish, and pain had been too much for her.

"Yes, she is innocent," said the eldest brother.

And now he told everything that had happened. And as he spoke a fragrance arose as of millions of roses, for every piece of wood in the pile had taken root and was sending forth shoots. There stood a fragrant hedge, tall and dense, covered with red roses, and at the top was a flower, white and shining, gleaming like a star. This flower the King plucked and placed in Eliza's bosom, and she awoke with peace and happiness in her heart.

And all the church bells began to ring, and the birds came in great flocks. And surely such a marriage procession that returned to the palace no King had ever seen before.

❦ Thumbelina ❧

THERE WAS ONCE A WOMAN who wished to have a tiny little child, but she did not know how to find one. So she went to an old witch.

"I yearn to have a little child! Can you tell me where I can find one?"

"Oh! That's easy," said the witch. "Here is a barleycorn. It's not the kind that grows in country fields, or that chickens eat. Plant it in a flowerpot, and you shall see what you shall see."

"Thank you," said the woman. She gave the witch a shiny coin and went home and planted the barleycorn. A lovely large flower that looked like a tulip sprouted up at once, the petals were tightly closed, as though it was still a bud.

"What a beautiful flower," said the woman and she kissed its pretty yellow-and-red petals. Just as she kissed it, the flower opened with a pop. It was a real tulip, but in the middle of the flower on the velvety green stamens sat a tiny girl. She was delicate and graceful, and a thumb high. So the woman called her Thumbelina.

A polished walnut shell was Thumbelina's cradle, her mattress was made of blue-violet leaves and she was covered by a rose leaf. She slept there at night, but in the daytime she played on the table, where the woman put a dish of water with a wreath of flowers around it. Thumbelina sailed around the dish on a large tulip leaf, using two fine white horsehairs as oars. And she would sing more sweetly than had ever been heard before.

One night, as she lay in her pretty bed, an old toad came hopping through a broken pane in the window. The toad was very ugly and big. It hopped right down onto the table where Thumbelina lay sleeping under the red rose leaf.

"That would be a lovely wife for my son," said the toad and she picked up the walnut shell in which Thumbelina lay asleep and hopped back through the window and down into the garden.

The toad and her son lived in the soft marshy bank of the broad brook that ran through the garden.

The son was ugly and gross, and looked just like his mother. "Kroaks, kroaks! Brekke-ke-keks!" That was all he could say when he saw the graceful little maiden in the walnut shell.

"Don't speak so loud, or she will wake up," said the old toad. "She might run away from us. We will put her out in the brook on one of the broad water lily leaves. It will be just like an island for her, she is so small and as light as swansdown. Then she can't run away while we put the best room under the marsh in order. That is where you are to live and keep house together."

A great many water lilies with broad green leaves that looked as if they were floating on the water grew in the brook. The leaf that was farthest out was the largest of all. The old toad swam out to the leaf and laid the walnut shell on it. When tiny Thumbelina woke early in the morning and saw where she was, she began to cry bitterly; there was water on all sides of the big green leaf, and she could not get to the land at all. The old toad worked down in the marsh, decking out her room with rushes and yellow waterweeds—she wanted it to be very pretty for her new daughter-in-law. When she was finished she and her ugly son swam out to the leaf where

Thumbelina was stranded. The old toad bowed low before her in the water.

"Here is my son. He will be your husband, and you will live happily together in the marsh."

"Kroaks, kroaks! Brekke-ke-keks!" was all her son could say.

Then they took the delicate walnut-shell bed and swam away with it. Thumbelina sat down, weeping bitterly; she did not want to live in the nasty toad's marsh, and have her ugly son for a husband. The fishes swimming in the brook had seen the toad and heard what she had said. They lifted their heads out of the water so that they could see the little girl. As soon as they saw how pretty she was, they felt very sorry that she should have to live with the vile toad. They all collected around the stalk that held the leaf on which she sat, and with their teeth they gnawed through the stalk so that the leaf floated downstream. Away went Thumbelina, far away where the toads could not get at her.

Thumbelina sailed by many towns, and the little birds in the bushes saw her, and sang "What a lovely little maiden!" The leaf was swept along with her, farther and farther, carrying Thumbelina through foreign lands.

A handsome white butterfly kept fluttering around her, and at last settled on the leaf. He had taken a fancy to Thumbelina, and she was very glad too, for now she knew the toads could not reach her. It was so beautiful where she was sailing—the sun shone on the rippling water, and it glittered like shining gold. She took her sash and tied one end of it to the butterfly, fastening the other end to the leaf making it glide on much faster.

Just then a stout brown maybug came flying past. He saw her, and in a flash seized her slender waist in his claws, and flew up into a tree. The green leaf went on swiftly downstream, carrying the distressed butterfly with it.

Thumbelina was so frightened, but most of all, she was worried about the charming white butterfly she had bound to the leaf, because if he could not free himself he would starve. The maybug, however, did not trouble himself at all about this. He sat down with her on the biggest leaf of the tree, offering her the sweet part of the flowers to eat, and declaring that she was very pretty, though not at all like a maybug. Soon all the other maybugs who lived in the tree came to pay a visit. They looked at Thumbelina and the young lady maybugs turned up their feelers and said, "Why, she has no more than two legs! How ungainly!"

"She doesn't have any feelers!" they said.

"Her waist is quite slender and she looks like a human creature, how ugly she is!" said all the lady maybugs.

The broad maybug who had carried her off had thought Thumbelina was beautiful. But when all the others said she was ugly he began to believe it and would not have her at all—she could go where she liked. They flew down with her and set her on a daisy. Thumbelina cried because the maybugs thought she was so ugly that they would have nothing to do with her. Yet she was the loveliest little being you could imagine, as tender and fair as the most beautiful rose petal.

The whole summer through poor Thumbelina lived all alone in the big forest. She braided a bed out of blades of grass and hung it up under a large burdock leaf so that she was protected from the rain. She sucked the honey out of the flowers for food, and drank the dew that stood on the leaves every morning. The summer and the autumn went by, then came the cold, long winter. All the birds who had sung so sweetly to her flew away, trees and flowers shed their leaves, the great burdock under which she had lived shrivelled up, leaving only a yellow withered stalk. She was dreadfully cold, her clothes were tattered, and she was so frail and small—poor Thumbelina, she was nearly frozen. It began to snow, and every snowflake that fell on her felt like a whole shovelful would feel to an ordinary person, for Thumbelina was tiny indeed. She tried wrapping herself up in a dry leaf, but that did not keep her warm, and she shivered with cold.

Just outside the forest she came to a huge cornfield, but the corn had gone long ago, only the naked dry stubble stood up out of the frozen ground. She was struggling through the field, when she came to the house of a field mouse. It was a little hole under the stubble. There the field mouse lived, warm and comfortable, with a whole roomful of corn, and a fine kitchen. Thumbelina stood at the door like a little urchin girl and begged for a bit of barleycorn. She had not had the smallest morsel to eat for two days.

"You poor little creature," said the kind old field mouse, "come into my warm house and have something to eat."

She liked Thumbelina and said, "If you want, you may stay with me through the winter, but you must keep my room clean and neat, and tell me lots of wonderful stories."

So Thumbelina stayed on with the old field mouse, and had a very good time.

"We shall have a visitor soon," said the field mouse one day. "My neighbour usually visits me once a week. He is even better off than

I am. He has a large house, and beautiful black velvety fur. If only you could get him for a husband, you would be well provided for, but he cannot see. You must tell him the most enchanting stories you know."

But Thumbelina did not care about the neighbour, who was a mole. He came and paid a visit in his black velvet pelt. The field mouse told her how rich and how wise he was, and how his house was more than twenty times larger than hers. She said that he was learned, but that he didn't like the sun or beautiful flowers, and sneered at them even though he had never seen them.

Thumbelina was asked to sing, and she sang both "Maybug, Fly, Fly Away!" and "The Monk Goes to the Field." The mole fell in love with her because of her beautiful voice, but he said nothing because he was a prudent mole.

A short time before his visit, the mole had dug a long underground passage from his own house to theirs. Thumbelina and the field mouse could use it as much as they wished. He begged them not to be afraid of the dead bird that was lying in the passage. It was a whole bird, with wings and a beak. It must have died when the winter began, and had been buried just where the mole had made his tunnel.

The mole put a piece of glowing tinder in his mouth, and led them through the long dark passage. When they came to the dead bird, the mole thrust his broad nose up against the ceiling and pushed the earth, so that a great hole was made for daylight to shine through. In the middle of the floor lay the dead swallow, his beautiful wings pressed close against his sides, his head and feet drawn back under his feathers. The bird had certainly died of the

cold. Thumbelina was very fond of all the little birds who had sung and twittered so sweetly for her through the summer, so she was saddened. But the mole poked the bird with his crooked legs and said, "Now he won't pipe anymore. It must be miserable to be born a little bird. I'm thankful that none of my children can do that. A bird has nothing but his 'tweet-tweet,' and starves in the winter."

"You are a very clever mole," observed the field mouse. "What use is all this 'tweet-tweet' to a bird when winter comes? He might still starve and freeze to death."

Thumbelina said nothing. When the two others had their backs turned, she bent down, brushed aside the feathers that covered his head, and kissed the bird on his closed eyes.

"Perhaps it was he who sang so beautifully last summer," she thought. "How much pleasure this lovely bird gave me."

The mole stopped up the hole through which the daylight shone, and took the ladies home. That night Thumbelina could not sleep at all. She got up out of her bed and wove a large soft carpet of hay. She crept down the passage to the dead bird and spread it over him. Then she laid some soft cotton wool that she had found in the field mouse's room at the bird's sides, so that he might be a little warmer lying there on the cold ground.

"Farewell, pretty little bird!" she said. "Farewell, and thanks for your beautiful song last summer when all the trees were green, and the sun shone down warmly on us." Then she gently laid her head on the bird's breast. But suddenly, she was startled, something was beating inside the bird. It was the bird's heart, he was not dead after all, only lying there in a deep, lifeless sleep, and now that he had been warmed, he came to life.

In the autumn, all the swallows fly away to warm countries. If one happens to be left behind, it becomes so cold that it falls down as if dead, and lies where it fell, the cold snow covering it over.

Thumbelina trembled all over, she was so surprised. Compared with her the bird was very, very large. She took courage, and pushed the cotton wool closer around the poor bird. Then she brought a leaf of mint that she had used as her own blanket, and put it over the bird's head.

The next night she stole down the passage again. Now the bird was alive, but so weak that he could only open his eyes for a moment and look wearily at Thumbelina, who stood next to him with a bit of tinder wood in her hand for light.

"Thank you, you pretty little child," said the sick swallow. "I feel so wonderfully warm. Soon I'll get my strength back and I will be able to fly out in the warm sunshine again."

"Oh," said Thumbelina, "it is so cold outside, the ground is frozen and covered with snow. Stay in your warm bed, and I will take care of you."

Then she brought the swallow water in a flower petal. He drank it, and told her how he had torn one of his wings in a thorn bush, and so had not been able to fly as fast as the other swallows, as they flew far, far away to the warm countries. At last he had fallen to the ground, but he couldn't remember anything, and didn't know at all how he had fallen into the passage.

He remained there for the whole winter and Thumbelina took care of him and grew very fond of him. She didn't tell the field mouse or the mole anything about it. As soon as the spring came and the sun warmed the earth, the swallow said good-bye to Thumbelina, and she opened the hole that the mole had made before. The sun shone in on them brightly. The swallow asked if Thumbelina would go away with him, she could sit on his back, and they would fly away into the green forest. But Thumbelina knew that the old field mouse would be terribly unhappy if she left her like this.

"I can't," said Thumbelina.

"Good-bye then, my sweet, lovely girl," said the swallow as he flew out into the sunshine. Thumbelina watched him go and the tears came into her eyes because she had become so fond of the dear swallow.

"Tweet-tweet, tweet-tweet," sang the bird, and he disappeared among the trees. Thumbelina felt very sad. She was not allowed to go out into the warm sunshine. The corn in the field over the house of the field mouse had grown high, it looked like dense woods to tiny Thumbelina.

"You must get your trousseau ready for your marriage this summer," said the field mouse. Their neighbour, the tiresome mole in the black velvet coat, had proposed to her. "You must have the finest wool and linen dresses. You shall have the best things to wear, and to sleep on too, when you are the mole's wife!"

Thumbelina had to have cloth, so the mole hired four spiders to weave for her day and night. Every evening the mole paid her a visit, and he was always complaining about the summer sun that was so hot, and about how it burned the earth almost as hard as stone. Then he would say that when the summer was over he would keep his wedding day with Thumbelina. But she was not happy at all. She didn't like the stuffy old mole. Every morning when the sun rose, and every evening when it went down, she sneaked out the door. When the wind blew the corn aside she could see the blue sky, and she thought how bright and beautiful it was and wished with all her heart to see her dear swallow again. But he did not come back; she thought he had flown far away into the beautiful green forest. When autumn came Thumbelina had all her wedding clothes ready.

"In four weeks we shall have your wedding!" said the field mouse.

But Thumbelina cried and said she would not marry the boring blind mole.

"Stuff and nonsense!" said the field mouse. "Don't be stubborn or I'll bite you with my sharp white teeth. He is a very fine mole to marry. The Queen herself doesn't have such a fine black velvet fur, and his kitchen and cellar are full. Be thankful to get him!"

So the wedding was to take place. The mole had already come to take Thumbelina home. She was to live with him deep under the ground, and never to come out into the warm sunshine that he so disliked. The little girl was miserably unhappy as she said farewell to the warm golden sun, which the field mouse had at last allowed her to go out and see.

"Good-bye bright sun," she said, and stretched up her hands to it as she walked a little way from the field mouse's house.

"Good-bye again!" she cried and she threw her little arms around a small red flower growing near. "Give my love to the dear swallow if you see him again."

"Tweet-tweet, tweet-tweet." She suddenly heard a familiar sound. She looked up and saw the swallow swooping overhead. As soon as he saw Thumbelina he was so happy. She told him how unwilling she was to marry the mole, who would make her live deep under the earth where the sun never shone. And she burst into tears.

"The cold winter is coming now," said the swallow. "I am going to fly far away to the warm countries. Will you come with me? You can sit upon my back. Tie yourself on with your sash, and we will fly away from the old mole and his dark room, far away over the mountains to a place where the sun shines brightly, where it is always summer, and there are lovely flowers. Fly with me, my dear Thumbelina, who saved my life when I lay frozen in the gloomy underground passage."

"Yes, I will go with you," said Thumbelina, and she climbed on the bird's back, with her feet on his outspread wing, and tied her sash tightly to one of his strongest feathers. Then the swallow flew high up into the air over the forest and sea, high up over the great snow-covered mountains. Thumbelina shivered in the cold air, so she crept under the bird's warm feathers, and only stuck out her little head to see all the beauty beneath her.

At last they reached the warm countries. The sun shone brilliantly, the sky was azure blue, plump, purple and green grapes grew on the vines, lemons and oranges ripened on the trees, the air was fragrant with the smell of herbs and fresh grass, and the loveliest children ran around, playing with large brightly coloured butterflies. But the swallow flew still farther, and it became even more and more beautiful. Under the magnificent green trees by a blue lake stood a palace of dazzling white marble. Vines wound themselves around the elegant pillars, and at the top were many swallows' nests. Here lived the good swallow who carried Thumbelina.

"That's my house," said the swallow. "But why don't you choose one of the lovely flowers growing below and I will put you safely into it, and you'll be as happy as you'll ever wish to be."

"How delightful," said she, and clapped her tiny hands.

A huge marble pillar had fallen and broken into three pieces, between them grew the most magnificent white flowers. The swallow flew down with Thumbelina, and put her on one of the broad petals. But what was her surprise! A little man sat in the middle of the flower, as transparent as if he had been made of glass and was no bigger than Thumbelina. He had a splendid gold crown on his head, and exquisite gleaming wings on his shoulders. He was the fairy angel of the flower. Tiny creatures just like him lived in each of the flowers, and he was the King of them all.

"Heavens, how beautiful he is," whispered Thumbelina to the swallow.

The small, delicate King was frightened when he saw the swallow. It looked like a giant bird to him. But when he saw Thumbelina he was overjoyed. She was the fairest maiden he had ever seen. He took the golden crown off his head and put it on hers, and asked if she would be his wife and Queen of all the flowers. He was very different from the ugly toad's son or the old mole with black velvet fur. So she said yes to the charming King. And from every flower came a pretty lady or a handsome gentleman. Each one brought Thumbelina a present, but the best of all was a pair of radiant wings from a butterfly. They were fastened to Thumbelina's back, so she too could fly from flower to flower. There was much rejoicing. The swallow sat above them in his nest, singing to them

as well as he could because he was so fond of Thumbelina that he would have liked her to stay with him forever.

"You shall not be called Thumbelina," said the flower angel; "it is not a pretty name, and you are so pretty. We will call you Maia."

"Farewell, farewell!" said the swallow, and he flew away from the warm countries, back to Denmark. There he had a little nest over the window where the man who can tell fairy tales lives. To him he sang "Tweet-tweet! Tweet-tweet!" and from that man we have the whole story.

The Elfin Hill

SOME LARGE LIZARDS were running nimbly around in the clefts of an old tree; they could understand one another very well, as they all spoke lizard.

"What a rumbling and buzzing there is in the old elfin hill!" one lizard said. "I haven't been able to close my eyes for two nights because of the noise! I might just as well be lying there with a toothache, for all the sleep I get!"

"There's something going on in there!" another lizard said. "They've been propping up the hill on four red posts until cock-crow, to air it out, and the elfin girls have learned new dances with some stamping in the steps! There's something going on."

"Yes, I was talking to an earthworm I know," said the third lizard. "The earthworm came right out of the hill, where he had been grubbing in the ground night and day; he had heard a great deal. He can't see, poor thing, but he understands how to wriggle around and listen. They expect visitors in the elfin hill—important visitors—but the earthworm couldn't tell me who they are, and in fact, it may be that he did not know himself. All the will-o'-the-wisps are ordered to hold what they call a torch dance; and the silver and gold, of which they have plenty in the elfin hill, are being polished and put out in the moonlight."

"Who do you think the strangers are?" asked the lizards. "What can be going on? Just listen to that noise, all that humming and rumbling!"

At that very moment the elfin hill opened, and an old elfin maiden, hollowed out in the back, but otherwise very respectably dressed, came dashing out. She was the old elfin king's housekeeper. A distant relative of the family, she wore an amber heart on her forehead. Her legs moved so quickly that you could barely make them out in the blur as she ran straight down to the moor, to the night raven.

"You are invited to the elfin hill this evening," she said, "but will you do me a great favour and deliver the invitations? You ought to do something, since you don't give parties yourself. We will have some very distinguished friends, troll folk who really have something to say; and so the old elfin king wants everything to be very impressive."

"Who's invited?" asked the night raven.

"Anyone in the world may come to the grand ball, even human beings, if they can talk in their sleep or do something in our way. But for the banquet the company is going to be very select; we will only have the most distinguished. I had an argument with the elfin king, for in my opinion we could not even admit ghosts. Before they get invited, we certainly have to invite the merman and his daughters. They may not be very happy at the thought of having to come onto dry land, but we'll give them a wet stone to sit on, or maybe something even better. I don't think they'll turn us down this time. We must have all the old trolls of the first class, with tails, and the wood demon and his gnomes; nor do I think we should leave out the grave pig, the death horse, and the church dwarf, although they belong to the clergy, who are not of our class. But that's only because of their work; they are closely

related to us, after all, and often come to call."

"Caw!" said the night raven, and flew off at once to deliver the invitations.

The elfin girls were already dancing on the elfin hill. They danced with long shawls woven of mist and moonlight, which looks very pretty if you like that sort of thing. In the middle of the elfin hall was the great hall, splendidly decorated. The floors had been washed with moonlight, and the walls rubbed with witches' fat; they shone in the light like tulips. In the kitchen plenty of frogs were roasting on the spit, snail skins wrapped around little children's fingers were laid out, all ready to be served, along with salads made from the noses of wet mice, mushroom spawn, and hemlock; beer brewed by the marsh witch, sparkling saltpeter wine from grave cellars—all a good solid banquet. The desserts included rusty nails and stained glass.

The old elfin king had his golden crown polished with powdered graphite, taken from the lead of pencils from the best schools. In the bedrooms, curtains were hung up, fastened with snail slime. Everyone was busy; giving each other advice and getting in the way.

"Now we must perfume the place by burning horsehair and pig bristles, and then I think we're all done," said the old elfin maiden.

"Father dear," said the youngest daughter, "now will you tell us who our distinguished guests are going to be?"

"Well," he said, "I suppose I have to tell you now. Two of my daughters must get ready to be married! The old goblin from Norway who lives in the old Dovrefjeld, and owns many strong castles up on those rocky hills, as well as a gold mine that is even better than most people know, is coming with his two sons, who both want to choose a wife. The old goblin is a true old honest Norwegian fighter, merry and straightforward. I know him from the old days when we used to drink together. He came here when he was looking for a wife; now she is dead—she was a daughter of the King of the Chalk-cliffs of Möen. They fell in love at first sight, as the saying goes. How I look forward to seeing that old Norwegian gnome! His sons, they say, are rather rude, forward youngsters, but perhaps people do them wrong, and they'll get better as they grow older. You might try to teach them some manners!"

"And when will they get here?" asked one of the daughters.

"That depends on the wind and weather," said the elfin king. "They travel economically: they come when there's a chance of a ship. I wanted them to go across Sweden, but the old one did not like the idea. He does not keep up with the times, and I don't like that."

Just then two will-o'-the-wisps came racing up, one quicker than the other, and so one came first.

"They're coming! They're coming!" they cried.

"Give me my crown, and let me stand in the moonlight," said the elfin king.

And the daughters lifted up their shawls and bowed down to the ground.

There stood the old goblin from Dovre, with a crown of hardened icicles and polished fir cones, wearing a bearskin and great warm boots. His sons, on the contrary, went bare-shouldered, and wore no armour, for they were strong men.

"Is that a hill?" asked the younger of the boys, who pointed to the elfin hill. "Up in Norway, we'd call that a hole."

"Boys!" said the old man, "a hole goes in, a hill goes up. Don't you have eyes in your heads?"

The only thing they thought was strange, they said, was that they could understand the language without difficulty.

"Don't put on airs!" said the old man. "You're acting like children!"

And then they went into the elfin hill, where the really grand company had assembled, in such haste that you might almost say they had been blown together. But it was comfortably and elegantly arranged for everyone. The sea folk sat at the table in big washtubs: they said it was just like being at home. Everyone showed their best table manners except the two small Northern trolls, who put their legs up on the table; but they thought they could get away with anything.

"Feet off of the table!" said the old goblin, and they obeyed, but not immediately. They tickled the ladies who sat next to them with pine cones that they'd brought along. Then they took off their boots to be more comfortable and gave them to the ladies to hold, but their father, the old Dovre goblin, was not at all like them. He told wonderful stories about the imposing Norwegian rocks and the waterfalls that rushed down, white with foam with a noise like thunder and the sound of organ music; he told about the salmon that leap up the rushing streams when the siren plays on her golden harp; he told about shining winter nights, when the sleigh bells are jingling and the boys skate with burning torches over the ice, which is so transparent that they can see the fishes move, startled, beneath their feet. He told it so well that you saw and heard what he described. It was just as if the sawmills were going, as if the servants

and maids were singing songs and dancing a wild dance. Then, all at once, the old goblin gave the old elfin girl a smacking kiss. And what a kiss that was! And they were not even related!

Then the elfin maidens had to dance, first in the usual way and then with stamping steps, which looked wonderful. Then came the artistic and solo dances. They really knew how to stretch their legs! Nobody knew where they began and where they ended, which were their arms and which their legs—they were all mixed up like wood shavings; and then they whirled around until the death horse got dizzy and had to leave the table.

"Lord!" cried the old goblin. "They certainly know how to move! But what else can they do besides dance, stretch their legs, and make a whirlwind?"

"You'll know soon!" said the elfin king.

And he called out the youngest of his daughters. She was as dainty and sweet as moonlight; she was the most delicate of all the sisters. She held a white shaving in her mouth and disappeared—that was her gift.

But the old goblin said he should not like his wife to possess this gift, and he did not think that his boys would, either.

The second daughter could walk next to herself, as if she had a shadow, which troll folk never have.

The third daughter was quite different; she had studied in the brewery of the marsh witch and understood how to layer elder tree logs with glowworms.

"She will make a good housewife," said the old goblin; and then he winked to her health with his eyes, as he did not want to drink too much.

Next came the fourth elfin girl; she had a big golden harp to play on. When she struck the first string, everyone there lifted up their left foot, for trolls are left-legged, and when she struck the second chord, everyone had to do what she wished.

"That's a dangerous woman!" said the old goblin; and both of his sons went outside of the hill, for they'd had enough.

"And what can the next daughter do?" asked the old goblin.

"I have learned to love everything that is Norwegian," she said, "and I will never marry unless I can go to Norway."

But the youngest sister whispered to the old king, "That's only because she has heard in a Norwegian song that when the world sinks down, the cliffs of Norway will remain standing like monuments, and so she wants to go there, because she is afraid of sinking down too."

"Aha!" said the old goblin. "Is that what it means? But what can the seventh and last do?"

"The sixth comes before the seventh!" said the elfin king, for he could count. But the sixth would not come out.

"I can only tell people the truth!" she said. "Nobody likes me, and I have enough to keep me busy, sewing my shroud."

Now came the seventh and last, and what could she do? She could tell stories, as many as she liked.

"Here are all my five fingers," said the old goblin. "Tell me one for each!"

And she took him by the wrist and told tales, and he laughed until he got red in the face. When she came to the ring finger, which had a golden ring around it, as if it knew already that there was going to be a wedding, the old goblin said:

"Hold on to what you have: the hand is yours; I'll have you for a wife myself!"

And the elfin girl said that the story of the ring finger and the baby finger were still to be told.

"We'll hear those in the winter," said the goblin, "and we'll hear about the pine tree, and the birch, and the fairies' presents, and the crackling frost. You shall tell your tales, because there is no one at all up there who knows how to do that well; and we'll sit in the stone rooms where the pine logs burn, and drink mead out of the golden horns left by the old Norwegian kings—the Neckan has given me a couple; and when we sit there, and the siren comes to visit, she'll sing you all her songs. That will be wonderful. The salmon will leap in the waterfall against the stone walls, but they can't come in.

"Oh, it's good to live in good old Norway; but where are my boys?"

Indeed, where were the boys? They were running around in the fields, and blowing out the will-o'-the-wisps, who had been kind enough to come for the torch dance.

"What's all this running around?" said the old goblin. "I have taken a mother for you, and now you may take one of the aunts."

But the boys said that they would rather make a speech and drink to friendship—they did not want to marry; so they made speeches, and drank to brotherhood, and turned their glasses upside down on their nails, to show that they had emptied them. Afterwards they took their coats off and lay down on the table to sleep; there was nothing formal about those boys. But the old goblin danced around the room with his young bride and changed boots with her,

which is more fashionable than exchanging rings.

"The cock is crowing," said the old elfin girl who kept house. "Now we have to shut the shutters, so the sun doesn't burn us."

And the hill shut itself up.

But outside the lizards ran up and down in the cleft of the tree, and one said to another:

"Oh, how much I like that old Norwegian goblin!"

"I like the boys better," said the earthworm. But he could not see, the miserable creature.

❧ Little Ida's Flowers ❧

"ALL MY FLOWERS HAVE DIED," said little Ida. "They were so pretty yesterday, and now all the leaves are withered. Why do they do that?" she asked the student who was sitting on the sofa with her. He was an amusing young man and she liked him very much because he knew how to tell the most beautiful stories, and could cut the most amusing pictures out of paper—hearts with little dancing ladies in them, flowers, and big castles with doors that opened. "Why do my flowers look so faded today?" she asked again, and showed him the bouquet which drooped sadly.

"Do you know what's the matter with them?" said the student. "The flowers were at a ball last night, and that's why they're hanging their heads."

"But flowers can't dance!" said little Ida.

"Oh, yes they can," said the student. "When it gets dark, and we're asleep, they jump merrily about. They go to a ball almost every night."

"Where do the beautiful flowers dance?" asked little Ida.

"Have you been outside the town gate, near the castle where the king lives in the summer, where there is a magnificent flower garden? That's where the splendid dances are held, believe me."

"I was out in that garden with my mother yesterday," said Ida, "but all the leaves are off the trees, and there are no longer any flowers there. Where are they? In the summer I saw so many!"

"They're in the castle," said the student. "As soon as the King and all the Court return to town, the flowers run out of the garden and into the castle to have the best time that they can. Just imagine it. The two most beautiful red roses sit on the throne and act as King and Queen. All the red cockscombs come and stand on each side of the throne and bow, they are the chamberlains. Then all the pretty flowers arrive and a grand ball begins. The blue violets represent little naval cadets, they dance with hyacinths and crocuses, whom they address most politely. The tall delphiniums and the tiger lilies are the old ladies who see that everyone dances well and behaves himself."

"But," asked Ida, "how come there's no one to stop the flowers from carrying on so wildly in the King's castle?"

"The truth is, nobody knows about it," said the young man. "Sometimes, of course, the old steward of the castle who keeps watch comes during the night. He has a big bunch of keys, so as soon as the flowers hear the keys rattle they fall silent and hide behind the curtains, and only occasionally poke their heads out. 'I can smell that there are flowers here,' the old steward says, but he can't see them."

"That's wonderful," little Ida said clapping her hands. "But why can't I see the flowers?"

"Why not," said the student, "when you go there again look through the window, and you will see them. I looked in today and saw a lovely yellow lily resting on the sofa and stretching her tired lily legs. She's a lady-in-waiting."

"Can the flowers from the Botanical Gardens go there? It is such a long way to go."

"Of course," said the student, "if they wish, they can fly. Haven't you seen dazzling butterflies, red, yellow, orange, and white? They look almost like flowers, and that is what they once were. They are flowers that learned to beat their petals like little wings and flew from their stalks high into the air. And because they behaved themselves well they got permission to fly about in the daytime too, and not return home to sit still on their stalks. Their petals became real wings. You have seen that yourself. But perhaps the flowers in the Botanical Gardens have never been to the King's castle and don't know that such wonderful parties go on at night. You could really surprise the botany professor who lives next door. When you go to his garden you must tell one of the flowers that a dancing party takes place at the castle every night, then that flower will tell all the others, and they will all fly away. When the professor comes into the garden he won't find a single flower there, and he'll be in a terrible state."

"But how can one flower tell the others? Flowers can't talk."

"Of course they can't," said the student, "but they can make signs. Haven't you ever noticed that when the wind blows a little the flowers nod to one another and move their green leaves? They understand each other as well as you and I when we talk to each other."

"Can the professor understand their signs?" asked Ida.

"Certainly. One morning he came into the garden and saw a large stinging nettle making signs with its leaves to a beautiful red carnation. It said, 'You are so pretty, and I love you with all my heart.' The professor can't stand things of that sort, and hit the stinging nettle on its leaves, which are its fingers, but then it bent forwards and stung him. Since that time he never dares touch a stinging nettle."

"What fun," said little Ida, smiling and laughing.

"How can you make the child believe such silly things," said the tiresome privy councillor, who had just arrived to pay a visit. He could not bear the witty student, and always grumbled when he saw him cutting out funny figures from paper. Sometimes the student cut out a man on a gallows holding a heart in his hand, who had been hanged for stealing hearts; sometimes he cut out an old witch, riding on a broomstick, and carrying her husband on her nose. The old privy councillor could not stand all this and he always said, as he did now, "How can you make a child believe such things? They are silly fantasies."

To little Ida what the student told her about the flowers seemed wonderfully possible, and she thought about it a great deal.

Her dying bouquet of flowers hung their heads because they were tired from dancing all night. Little Ida understood that now. So she took them to meet her toys, which were kept on a small table that had a whole drawer full of pretty things. Her doll Sophy was sleeping in the doll's bed, but little Ida said to her, "You must get up now, Sophy, and be content to sleep in the drawer tonight. The flowers are ill, and they should rest in your bed. Perhaps then they will recover." She took Sophy out at once, the doll looked very cross but did not say a single word.

Ida gently put the flowers in the doll's bed and pulled the paisley quilt over them. She said they must lie quietly, and she would make them some tea, so that they would get better and be able to get up in the morning. She drew the flocked curtains around the bed, so

that the sun wouldn't shine on them. Before Ida got into bed herself, she looked at the windowsill where her mother's beautiful hyacinths and tulips stood, and she whispered in a low voice, "I know
where you're going tonight—to the ball." The flowers pretended
not to understand her, and did not stir a leaf, but little Ida knew
what she knew.

When she had gone to bed she lay awake for a long time thinking
how delightful it would be to see the flowers dancing in the King's
ballroom. "I wonder if my flowers have really been there?" Then
she fell asleep. During the night she woke up; she had been dreaming of the flowers and of the student whom the privy councillor had
scolded. It was very quiet in the bedroom where Ida slept, the
night-light was burning on the table, and the rest of the family was
fast asleep.

"I wonder if my flowers are still sleeping in Sophy's bed," she
thought. "I'd really like to know!" She looked towards the door
which was ajar; her flowers and all her toys were just behind it. She
listened, and it seemed to her as if she heard someone playing the
piano very softly and more beautifully than she had ever heard before. "I am sure all my flowers are dancing in there," she thought.
"How I'd like to see them." But she was afraid of waking her father
and mother.

"I wish they would come in here," she murmured. The flowers
did not come, but the tinkling music played on. Ida was so curious,
she couldn't bear staying in bed any longer. She crept softly towards
the door and peered into the room. There was no night-light, but
moon beams were bouncing brightly on the walls and floor. All the
hyacinths and tulips stood in two long rows, not one remained in

the flowerpots on the windowsill. The flowers danced gracefully around one another, holding each other by their long green leaves swaying and swinging. A plump golden lily sat at the piano. Little Ida was certain she had seen it in the summer, she remembered distinctly that the student had said, "How much that lily is like Miss Lina, the music mistress." They all had laughed at him, but now it seemed to little Ida that the flower was really like Miss Lina. The lily played in just the same way, bending her smiling yellow head over the piano keys, nodding in time to the music. No one noticed little Ida. Then she saw a big blue crocus jump on the table, walk straight to the doll's bed, and pull the curtain away. The sick flowers were there, but they got up quickly and sprang to the dance floor, bobbing their brightly coloured heads, ready to join in the fun. They were totally recovered. The old nutcracker, shaped like a man whose lower jaw was broken off, bowed to the newcomers, welcoming them to the party.

Suddenly it seemed as if something fell from the table. Ida looked and saw the carnival birch rod jump down. It was made of birch twigs tied together, decorated with lovely little ornaments. In Denmark, the younger children in the family each get one just before Easter. It looked very pretty, and a little wax doll with a broad-brimmed hat, like the one the privy councillor usually wore, sat on it. The carnival birch rod hopped about among the flowers on its twiggy legs and stamped loudly as it danced a mazurka. The other flowers couldn't manage such a dance because they were too light and had no feet to stamp.

The wax doll on the carnival birch rod suddenly grew and, standing over the paper flowers that were also on the rod, exclaimed,

"How can you make a child believe such silly fantasies?" The wax doll looked exactly like the privy councillor—nasty and cross. But the paper flowers hit him on his thin legs, and he shrank back to a little wax doll. Ida was enthralled and could not help laughing. The carnival birch rod continued to dance, so the privy councillor had to dance too. There was no getting out of it, whether he made himself tall or remained the little wax doll with the broad-brimmed black hat. Finally the other flowers, especially the bouquet that had been so sick, asked the carnival birch rod to stop. At the same moment there was a loud knocking in the drawer where Sophy lay with the other toys. The nutcracker walked up to the edge of the table and began to open the drawer. Sophy looked up with astonishment. "Is there a ball here tonight?" she said. "Why didn't anyone tell me?"

"Will you dance with me?" said the nutcracker.

"I won't dance with a broken nutcracker," she said, and turned her back on it.

Then she sat down on the edge of the drawer and hoped that one of the flowers would ask her to dance, but none did. She coughed and made little noises to attract attention, but even so no one asked her to dance. Then the nutcracker began to dance by itself, and it really danced quite well. Sophy let herself drop down from the drawer to the floor with a loud plop. All the flowers came running to her and asked if she had hurt herself. They were all very polite to her, especially the flowers who had slept in her bed. But she was not hurt, and Ida's flowers thanked her for the beautiful bed, and they were very kind to her. They took her into the middle of the room, where the moon was shining most brightly, and danced with her, while all the other flowers made a circle around them. Now Sophy was happy, and she told the flowers that they could sleep in her bed as long as they wanted, she would not mind sleeping in the drawer.

But the flowers said, "You are very kind, but we won't live much longer, we shall be all withered by tomorrow. Tell little Ida to bury us in the garden where she has buried her dear canary, then we shall wake up again next summer and be more radiant than ever."

"No, you must not die," said Sophy, and kissed them. Then the door flew open and hundreds of beautiful flowers came dancing in. Ida didn't know where they came from, perhaps from the King's castle. Two glorious roses with crowns on their heads walked in front, they were King and Queen. Then came gladiolus and carnations, bowing to all sides. They had brought an orchestra with them. White poppies and pink peonies blew on pea pods until they were quite red in the face. The buttercups and the fragile white lilies-of-the-valley tinkled as if they had bells. Many other flowers came, and they all danced—marigolds, daffodils, hollyhocks, snap-dragons, and even exotic orchids. At last all the flowers kissed one another and said good-night. Then little Ida tiptoed back to her bed and dreamed of all she had seen. When she got up in the morning, she quickly went to the small table to see if her flowers were still there. She pulled back the curtains from the little bed and there they lay, all withered—much more so than the day before. Sophy was lying in the drawer where Ida had put her, but she looked unusually tired.

"Can you remember what you have to tell me?" asked little Ida. Sophy did not say a single word. "You are not very nice," said Ida.

"Didn't they all dance with you?" She took a small paper box decorated with lovely birds, and put the dead flowers in it. "This will be your resting place," she said, "and when my Norwegian cousins come again they will help me bury you out in the garden, and next summer you will grow again and be prettier than ever!"

The Norwegian cousins were two friendly boys named Jonas and Adolph, and when they came they brought their new crossbows with them to show to Ida. She told them about the withered flowers and asked them to help her bury them. The two boys walked in front with their crossbows on their shoulders, while little Ida followed carrying the paper box with the dead flowers. They dug a little grave in the garden. Ida kissed the flowers, closed the box, and placed it in the soft ground. Adolph and Jonas shot their crossbows over the grave as a farewell salute to the flowers that had danced so merrily for dear little Ida.

❧ The Emperor's New Clothes ❧

MANY YEARS AGO there lived an Emperor who was so fond of new clothes that he spent all his money on them. He did not care for his soldiers, or for the theatre, or for driving in the woods, except to show off his new clothes. He had an outfit for every hour of the day, and just as they say of a king, "He is in the council chamber," so they always said of him, "The Emperor is in his dressing room."

The great city where he lived was very lively, and every day many strangers came there. One day two swindlers came. They claimed that they were weavers and said they could weave the finest cloth imaginable. Their colours and patterns, they said, were not only exceptionally beautiful, but the clothes made of this material possessed the wonderful quality of being invisible to any man who was unfit for his office, or who was hopelessly stupid.

"Those must be wonderful clothes," thought the Emperor. "If I wore them, I should be able to find out which men in my empire were unfit for their posts, and I could tell the clever from the stupid. Yes, I must have this cloth woven for me without delay." So he gave a lot of money to the two swindlers in advance, so that they could set to work at once.

They set up two looms and pretended to be very hard at work, but they had nothing on the looms. They asked for the finest silk and the most precious gold, all of which they put into their own bags, and worked at the empty looms till late into the night.

"I should very much like to know how they are getting on with the cloth," thought the Emperor. But he felt rather uneasy when he remembered that whoever was not fit for his office could not see it. He believed, of course, that he had nothing to fear for himself, yet he thought he would send somebody else first to see how things were progressing.

Everybody in the town knew what a wonderful property the stuff possessed, and all were anxious to see how bad or stupid their neighbours were.

"I will send my honest old minister to the weavers," thought the Emperor. "He can judge best how the stuff looks, for he is intelligent, and nobody is better fitted for his office than he."

So the good old minister went into the room where the two swindlers sat working at the empty looms. "Heaven help us!" he thought, and opened his eyes wide. "Why, I cannot see anything at all," but he was careful not to say so.

Both swindlers bade him be so good as to step closer, and asked him if he did not admire the exquisite pattern and the beautiful colours. They pointed to the empty looms, and the poor old minister opened his eyes even wider, but he could see nothing, for there was nothing to be seen. "Good Lord!" he thought, "can I be so stupid? I should never have thought so, and nobody must know it! Is it possible that I am not fit for my office? No, no, I must not tell anyone that I couldn't see the cloth."

"Well, have you got nothing to say?" said one, as he wove.

"Oh, it is very pretty—quite enchanting!" said the old minister, peering through his glasses. "What a pattern, and what colours! I shall tell the Emperor that I am very much pleased with it."

"Well, we are glad of that," said both the weavers, and they described the colours to him and explained the curious pattern. The old minister listened carefully, so that he might tell the Emperor what they said.

Now the swindlers asked for more money, more silk and more gold, which they required for weaving. They kept it all for themselves, and not a thread came near the loom, but they continued, as before, working at the empty looms.

Soon afterwards the Emperor sent another honest official to the weavers to see how they were getting on, and if the cloth was nearly finished. Like the old minister, he looked and looked, but could see nothing, as there was nothing to be seen.

"Is it not a beautiful piece of cloth?" said the two swindlers, showing and explaining the magnificent pattern, which, however, was not there at all.

"I am not stupid," thought the man, "so it must be that I am unfit for my high post. It is ludicrous, but I must not let anyone know it." So he praised the cloth, which he did not see, and expressed his pleasure at the beautiful colours and the fine pattern. "Yes, it is quite enchanting," he said to the Emperor.

Everybody in the whole town was talking about the beautiful cloth. At last the Emperor wished to see it himself while it was still on the loom. With a whole company of chosen courtiers, including the two honest councillors who had already been there, he went to the two clever swindlers, who were now weaving away as hard as they could, but without using any thread.

"Is it not magnificent?" said both the honest statesmen. "Look, your Majesty, what a pattern! What colours!" And they pointed to the empty looms, for they imagined the others could see the cloth.

"What is this?" thought the Emperor. "I do not see anything at all. This is terrible! Am I stupid? Am I unfit to be Emperor? That would indeed be the most dreadful thing that could happen to me!"

"Yes, it is very beautiful," said the Emperor. "It has our highest approval," and nodding contentedly, he gazed at the empty loom, for he did not want to say that he could see nothing. All the attendants who were with him looked and looked, and, although they could not see anything more than the others, they said, just like the Emperor, "Yes, it is very fine." They all advised him to wear the new magnificent clothes at a great procession that was soon to take place. "It is magnificent! beautiful, excellent!" went from mouth to mouth, and everybody seemed delighted. The Emperor awarded each of the swindlers the cross of the order of knighthood to be worn in their buttonholes, and the title of Imperial Court Weavers.

Throughout the night preceding the procession, the swindlers were up working, and they had more than sixteen candles burning. People could see how busy they were getting the Emperor's new clothes ready. They pretended to take the cloth from the loom, they snipped the air with big scissors, they sewed with needles without any thread, and at last said: "Now the Emperor's new clothes are ready!"

The Emperor, followed by all his noblest courtiers, then came in. Both the swindlers held up one arm as if they held something, and said: "See, here are the trousers! Here is the coat! Here is the cloak!" and so on. "They are all as light as a cobweb! They make one feel as if one had nothing on at all, but that is just the beauty of it."

"Yes!" said all the courtiers, but they could not see anything, for there was nothing to see.

"Will it please your Majesty graciously to take off your clothes?" said the swindlers. "Then we may help your Majesty into the new clothes before the large mirror!"

The Emperor took off all his clothes, and the swindlers pretended to put on the new clothes, one piece after another. Then the Emperor looked at himself in the glass from every angle.

"Oh, how well they look! How well they fit!" said all. "What a pattern! What colours! Magnificent indeed!"

"They are waiting outside with the canopy which is to be borne over your Majesty in the procession," announced the master of the ceremonies.

"Well, I am quite ready," said the Emperor. "Doesn't my suit fit me beautifully?" And he turned once more to the mirror so that people would think he was admiring his garments.

The chamberlains, who were to carry the train, fumbled with their hands on the ground as if they were lifting up a train. Then they pretended to hold something up in their hands. They didn't dare let people know that they could not see anything.

And so the Emperor marched in the procession under the beautiful canopy, and all who saw him in the street and out of the windows exclaimed: "How marvellous the Emperor's new suit is! What a long train he has! How well it fits him!" Nobody would let the others know that he saw nothing, for then he would have been

shown to be unfit for his office or too stupid. None of the Emperor's clothes had ever been such a success.

"But he has nothing on at all," said a little child.

"Good heavens! Hear what the innocent child says!" said the father, and then each whispered to the other what the child said: "He has nothing on—a little child says he has nothing on at all!" "He has nothing on at all," cried all the people at last. And the Emperor too was feeling very worried, for it seemed to him that they were right, but he thought to himself, "All the same, I must go through with the procession." And he held himself stiffer than ever, and the chamberlains walked on, holding up the train which was not there at all.

The Little Match Girl

IT WAS TERRIBLY COLD; it was snowing and almost dark. It was also the last evening of the year. In the cold and darkness a poor little girl, with bare head and naked feet, went along the streets. When she had left home, it is true, she had had slippers on, but what good were they? They were very large; big enough for her mother to wear. The little girl lost them as she hurried across the street to get out of the way of two carts driving furiously along. One slipper was not to be found again, and a boy had picked up the other and had run away with it. He said he could use it for a cradle when he had children of his own! So the little girl had to go walking in her bare feet, which were blue with cold. She carried a lot of matches in an old apron and a box of them in her hand. No one had bought any from her the whole day; no one had given her so much as a penny.

Hungry and shivering, she went along, poor little thing, a picture of misery.

The snowflakes fell on her long yellow hair that curled so prettily on her neck, but she did not think of that now. Lights were shining in all the windows, and there was a tempting smell of roast goose, for it was New Year's Eve. Yes, she was thinking of that.

In a corner formed by two houses, one of which projected a little beyond the other, she sat down and huddled against the cold. She had tucked her feet under her, but she felt colder and colder. She didn't dare go home, for she had not sold any matches nor earned a single penny, and her father would beat her. Anyway, it was cold at home: they had only the roof above them, through which the wind whistled, although the largest cracks had been stopped up with straw and rags.

Her hands were almost dead with cold. Ah! One little match might do her good! If she dared take only one out of the box, strike it on the wall, and warm her fingers! She took one out and struck it. How it sputtered and burned!

It was a warm, bright flame, like a little candle, when she held her hands over it. It was a wonderful little light, and it really seemed to the child as though she were sitting in front of a great iron stove with polished brass feet and brass ornaments. How the fire burned, and how it warmed! But what was that? The little girl was already stretching out her feet to warm them too, when—out went the little flame, the stove vanished, and she had only the remains of the burned match in her hand.

She struck a second one on the wall; it burned and gave a light, and where the light fell on the wall it became transparent, like a veil—she could see right into the room. A white tablecloth was spread upon the table, which was decked with shining china dishes, and there was a lovely smell of roast goose stuffed with apples and prunes. What pleased the poor little girl more than anything was that the goose hopped down from the dish and came waddling across the floor straight towards her. Just at that moment, out went the match, and only the thick, cold wall was to be seen. So she lighted another match. And there she was sitting under the beautiful Christmas tree; it was much larger and more decorated than the one she had seen through the glass doors at the rich merchant's. The green boughs were lit up with thousands of candles, and gaily painted figures, like those in the shop windows, looked down on her. The little girl stretched her hands out towards them and—out went the match. The Christmas candles rose higher and higher, till they were only the stars in the sky; one of them fell, leaving a long fiery trail behind it.

"Now, someone is dying," said the little girl, for her old grandmother, the only person who had ever been good to her and who was now dead, had said that when a star falls a soul goes up to heaven.

She struck another match on the wall; it lighted immediately and in its glow stood her old grandmother, so dazzling and bright, and so kind and loving.

"Grandmother!" cried the little girl. "Oh, please take me with you! I know that you will go away when the match goes out; you will vanish like the warm stove and the beautiful roast goose and the lovely big Christmas tree."

She quickly lighted the whole box of matches, for she did not wish to let her grandmother go. The matches burned with such a blaze that it was lighter than day, and the old grandmother had never appeared so beautiful or so tall before. Taking the little girl in her arms she flew up with her in brightness and joy, high, so high; and there was no cold, or hunger, or sorrow—for they were with God.

But in the corner by the houses, in the cold dawn, the little girl was still sitting, with red cheeks and a smile on her lips—frozen to

death on the last evening of the old year. The new year's sun shone down on the little body. The child sat up stiffly, holding her matches, of which a box had been burned.

"She must have tried to warm herself," someone said.

No one knew what beautiful things she had seen, nor into what glory she had entered with her grandmother on the joyous New Year.

✷ The Ugly Duckling ✷

IT WAS A DELIGHTFUL SUMMER out in the country. The cornfields were golden, the oats were green, the meadows were dotted with sweet-smelling haystacks, and the stork went about on his long red legs, chattering in Egyptian, the language he had learned from his mother. Near the fields and meadows was a large forest, and in the middle of the forest were deep, dark blue lakes. An old manor house, surrounded by deep canals, stood at the forest's edge, and from its walls down to the water grew gardens with enormous burdocks, so high that little children could stand straight up under the tallest of them. It was as wild as in the deepest part of the forest. A mother duck sat there on her nest. She had to hatch her ducklings, but she was almost totally tired out, because it was taking such a long time, and no one came to visit her. The other ducks would rather swim around in the canals than climb up, sit under a burdock, and quack with her.

At last, one egg after another cracked open. "Peep! Peep!" they cried; all the yolks had come to life, and little heads were peering out.

"Quack! Quack!" said the duck, and they all came out quacking as fast as they could, looking all around them under the green leaves. Their mother let them look as much as they wished, because green is good for newly hatched duckling eyes.

"How wide the world is!" said the young ones. They had so much more room now than when they were in their eggshells.

"Don't think this is the whole world," said the mother. "There's much more that stretches to the other side of the garden, through the meadows and into the leafy forest; but I have never been that far. I hope you are all hatched now," she said, and stood up to count the ducklings. "No I haven't got you all. The biggest egg is still there. How long is this going to last? I am getting very tired." And she sat down again.

"Well, well, how are you?" said an old duck, who had finally come to pay her a visit.

"It's taking so long for that last egg to hatch," said the mother duck, sitting there impatiently. "It won't crack. But look at all the others! They're the prettiest fluffy ducklings I have ever seen! They are just like their father, the rascal! He never comes to see me."

"Let me see the egg that won't crack," said the old one. "I'll bet that it's a turkey egg! I was once cheated that way, and had a lot of bother and trouble with the young ones because they are afraid of the water. I couldn't get them into it. I quacked and pecked, but it was no use. Let me see the egg. Yes, that's a turkey egg! Leave it alone, and just teach the other children to swim."

"I think I'll just sit on it a little longer," said the duck. "I've sat so long now that I might as well sit a few more days."

"As you please," said the old duck, and she waddled away.

At last the egg broke. "Peep! Peep!" it said, and crept out. It was very big and very ugly. The duck stared at it.

"That's terribly big for a duckling," she said. "None of the others look like that. Can it really be a turkey chick? Well, we will soon find out. He's going into the water, even if I have to push him in myself!"

Next day the weather was warm, and the sun shone brightly on the thick green burdocks. The mother duck went down to the canal with all her little ones. With a splash she sprang into the water. "Quack! Quack!" she said, and one duckling after another threw itself in. The water closed over their heads, but they bobbed right up again and swam beautifully; their legs churned all by themselves. There they were, all in the water, and the ugly duckling was swimming with them.

"No, he's not a turkey," she said. "See how well he uses his legs and how he holds himself straight. He's my own child! Really, he's quite pretty if you look at him the right way. Quack! Quack! Come along with me, and I'll lead you out into the world and present you to the poultry yard. Keep close to me, so no one walks on you, and watch out for the cats!"

And so they came into the poultry yard. There was an awful riot going on there. Two families were fighting over an eel's head, and in the end, the cat got it.

"See, that's the way the world is!" said the mother duck; and she whetted her beak, for she had wanted the eel's head, too. "Just use your legs," she said. "Make sure that you bustle around, and bow your heads before the old duck over there. She's the greatest of them all and has royal Spanish blood—that's why she's so fat. Look at the red rag around her leg. That's the greatest distinction possible for a duck; it means that she can be recognized by man and beast wherever she goes and no one will lose her. Now get going—don't turn in your toes! A well-brought-up duck turns its toes out, just like his father and mother—like so! Now bend your necks and say 'Quack!' "

And so they did; but the other ducks around looked at them, and said out loud:

"Look over there! Now we're going to have that bunch too, as if there weren't enough of us already! And look how ugly that duckling is! We won't take that!" And one of the mean, mottled ducks flew straight at him, and bit him on the neck.

"Let him alone," said the mother, "he's doing no harm to anyone."

"Yes, but he's too big and so different," said the duck who had bitten him, "that we must peck at him."

"Those are pretty children that mother over there has!" said the old duck with the rag on her leg. "They're all lovely except that one; he's so gawky! I wish she could hatch him all over again."

"That cannot be your Highness," said the duckling's mother. "He is not handsome, but he has an even temper, and he swims as well as any other—I might even say better! I think he will grow pretty, and may become smaller in time! He was in his shell too long and doesn't have the proper shape." And she stroked his neck and smoothed his feathers. "But after all, he is a drake," she said, "and so it doesn't matter as much. I think he will grow to be very strong, and be able to make his own way in the world."

"The other ducklings are graceful enough," said the old duck. "Make yourself at home; and if you find an eel's head you may bring it to me."

Now they felt at home. But the poor duckling who was the last out of his egg, who looked so ugly, was bitten and pushed and teased by most of the ducks and other poultry.

"He is too big!" they all said. And the turkey cock, who had been born with spurs and thought he was an emperor, puffed himself up like a ship in full sail and turned on the ugly duckling, gobbling fiercely and growing red in the face. The poor duckling did not know where to stand or where to swim. He was absolutely miserable because he looked ugly and was the butt of the whole yard.

So it went the first day, and afterwards it only got worse. The poor duckling was taunted by all of them. Even his brothers and sisters were mean to him and said, "I hope the cat catches you, you ugly thing!" And his mother said, "If only you were far away!" The ducks bit him, the chickens pecked at him, and the girl who fed the poultry even kicked him.

Then he beat his large wings and flew over the hedge, and the little birds in the bushes hurried away in fear.

"It's because I am so ugly!" thought the duckling. He shut his eyes, but went on farther, until he came to a great marsh where the wild ducks lived. He lay there the whole night long—he was so tired and unhappy.

Towards morning the wild ducks flew up and looked at their new comrade.

"What kind of duck are you?" they asked. The duckling turned in every direction and bowed to them as well as he could. "You are remarkably ugly!" said the wild ducks. "But that doesn't make any difference to us, as long as you don't marry into our family!"

Poor thing! He certainly wasn't thinking of marrying, and only hoped to be allowed to lie among the reeds and drink some of the marsh water.

He had been there three whole days, when two wild geese came, or rather, ganders, since they both were males. They had only come out of their eggs quite recently, which is why they were so bold and impudent.

"Listen, comrade," one of them said. "You're so ugly that I like you. Why don't you come with us? Near here, in another marsh, there are a few lovely wild geese, all unmarried, and all able to say 'Quack!' You've got a real chance of making your fortune, even as ugly as you are!"

"Bang! Bang!" sounded in the air above, and the two ganders fell dead in the swamp, and the water stained blood-red. "Bang! Bang!" it sounded again, and whole flocks of wild geese rose up from the reeds. And then there was another shot. The hunters were lying in wait all around the marsh; some were even sitting up in the branches of the trees that stretched far over the reeds. Blue smoke rose up like clouds among the dark trees and drifted far across the water. The hunting dogs ran through the rushes and reeds, breaking and bending them. The poor duckling was petrified. He turned his head and put it under his wing, but at that moment a huge, terrible dog stopped right next to him. The dog's tongue hung far out of his mouth and his eyes gleamed wildly. He thrust out his nose close to the duckling, bared his sharp teeth, and then—on he went, without touching the duckling.

"Oh, thank heaven!" sighed the duckling. "I am so ugly that the dog doesn't even want to bite me!"

He sat quite still while the shots rattled through the reeds, and gun after gun went off. At last, late in the day, all was quiet again. The scared duckling did not dare to move; he waited several hours before he looked around, and then got out of the marsh as fast as he could. He ran on, through fields and meadows, while a terrible storm was blowing, making it even more difficult to get away.

Towards evening the duckling came to a small, forlorn peasant's hut. It was so tumbledown that it didn't know which side should fall in first, which is the only reason it still stood. The storm whistled so fiercely around the duckling that he had to sit down to withstand it. As the tempest grew worse and worse, the duckling noticed that one of the hinges of the door had given way, and the door hung so crookedly that he could slip through the crack into the room.

A woman lived there with her tomcat and her hen. The tomcat could arch his back and purr, and he would even give out sparks if you stroked his fur the wrong way. The hen had very little, short legs; she laid good eggs and the woman loved her as her own child.

In the morning they noticed the strange duckling at once, and the tomcat began to purr, and the hen to cluck.

"What's all this?" said the woman, as she looked around. But she could not see very well, and so she thought the duckling was a fat duck that had strayed in. "This is a rare catch!" she said. "Now I'll have duck eggs. I hope it is not a drake. Well, we'll find that out."

And so the duckling was allowed to stay for three weeks, but no eggs came. The tomcat was master of the house, and the hen was mistress, and she always said, "It's us against the world!" She actually thought that they were half the world, and by far the better half, too. The duckling thought that it might be possible to have a different opinion, but the hen would not allow it.

"Can you lay eggs?" she asked.

"No."

"Then you'd better hold your tongue."

And the tomcat said, "Can you arch your back, and purr, and give out sparks?"

"No."

"Then you shouldn't have any opinions of your own when sensible cats and hens are talking."

The duckling sat sadly in a corner, but when the fresh air and the sunshine streamed in, he was seized with such a strong longing to swim in the water that he couldn't help telling the hen about it.

"What are you thinking about?" cried the hen. "You have nothing to do, that's why you have these fantasies. Lay eggs or purr and they will go away."

"But it's so delightful to swim," said the duckling, "so glorious to let the water flow over your head, and dive down to the bottom!"

"Yes, I'm sure that's a great pleasure," said the hen. "You must be going crazy. Ask the cat about it—he's the wisest creature I know— ask him if he likes to swim in the water or dive under it. I won't talk about my own feelings. Ask our mistress, the old woman, no one in the world is wiser than she is. Do you think that she has any desire to swim and let the water flow over her head?"

"You don't understand me," said the duckling.

"We don't understand you? Then tell me who will? You surely don't pretend to be wiser than the tomcat and the old woman—to say nothing of myself? Don't be conceited, child, and be grateful for all the kindness that we've shown you. Here you are, in a warm room, with others who can teach you something. But you talk too much, and it's no fun to be with you. Believe me, I speak for your own good. I may say unpleasant things to you, but that is the way you know who your real friends are! Take my advice: Learn to lay eggs, or how to purr and give off sparks!"

"I think I'll go out into the wide world," said the duckling.

"Well then, go ahead if you want to," said the hen.

The duckling went away quickly. He dove in the water and swam, but still all the other animals stayed away from him because he was gangly and gawky and not handsome at all.

Then autumn came. The leaves in the forest turned yellow and brown, and as the wind caught them, they danced around. The air turned sharply cold. The clouds hung low, heavy with hail and snow, and on the fence, a raven croaked "Caw! Caw!" from sheer cold. The duckling was having a terrible time. But then, one evening just as the sun was setting in all its fiery beauty, a whole flock of great handsome birds came out of the bushes. The duckling had never seen anything so beautiful. They were dazzlingly white, with long, slender necks. They were swans and uttered a very peculiar cry, as they spread their lovely long wings and flew away from that bitter cold place to warmer lands with open lakes. They rose so high that the ugly little duckling felt very strange as he watched them. He turned around and around in the water like a wheel, stretched out his neck towards them, and uttered such a strange loud cry that he even frightened himself.

He could not forget those beautiful birds that looked so happy; and as soon as they disappeared in the sky, he dived straight down to the bottom. When he came up again he was beside himself with confusion and unhappiness. He didn't know what kind of birds they were, or where they were flying; but he loved them more than he had ever loved anything before. He wasn't envious of them at all.

How could he imagine even wishing for the beauty they had? He would have been quite happy if even the ducks would have allowed him to stay with them.

As the winter grew colder, the duckling was forced to swim around in the water to keep it from freezing over. Every night the hole he swam in became smaller and smaller. It froze so hard that the icy covering cracked and the duckling had to use his legs all the time to keep the hole from freezing up completely. At last he became exhausted. He lay very still, and soon he froze fast into the ice.

Early in the morning a peasant came by and saw him. He took his wooden shoe and broke the ice, and then carried the duckling home to his wife. In the warm house the duck revived. The children wanted to play with him, and in his fright he fluttered up into the milk pan and splashed milk all over the room. Then, when the woman cried out and clapped her hands, the duckling flew into the butter tub, and then into the meal barrel. What a sight he was! The woman screamed, and struck at him with the fire tongs. The children tumbled over each other, trying to catch the duckling; and they laughed and shrieked. Fortunately the door stood open, so the butter-smeared, meal-coated duckling was able to slip out among the shrubs covered with newly fallen snow.

It would be too sad to tell you all the misery and hardship that the duckling endured through that hard winter. Then one day the sun began to shine warmly again. The larks were singing for the first time and it was truly springtime.

All at once the duckling flapped his wings. They beat the air more strongly than before, and he flew away quickly. Before he knew it, he found himself in a large garden where the apple trees blossomed and lilacs scented the air and lavender wisteria grew down to the winding canals. Everything was radiant in the fresh spring air. From the thicket right in front of him came three lovely white swans ruffling their feathers as they swam lightly over the water. The duckling knew the splendid creatures and was seized with a strange sadness.

"If I fly over to these regal birds they will surely kill me because I am so ugly and I have dared to go near them. But that does not matter! Better to be killed by them than snapped at by ducks, or pecked at by nasty fowls, or kicked by the girl who takes care of the poultry yard, or suffer from hunger in the winter!" And he flew into the water and swam towards the beautiful swans. They saw him and came sailing up, their feathers fanned out. "Kill me!" said the ugly duckling, and he bent his head down to the water, waiting for his death. But when he saw his image reflected in the clear water, he could barely believe his eyes. He was no longer a clumsy, dark gray bird, ugly and ungainly—he was a splendid white swan.

It doesn't matter if you're born in a duck yard if you come from the egg of a swan.

All the misfortune and trouble he had suffered seemed worthwhile now that he realized his good fortune to have all the beauty that surrounded him. The big swans swam around him and stroked him with their beaks.

Some little children came into the garden. They threw bread and corn into the water, and the youngest cried, "There is a new one!" Then the other children shouted with joy, "Yes, a new one has come!" They clapped their hands and danced around, and ran

to their father and mother to get bread and cake to throw into the water. The whole family said, "The new one is the most beautiful of all. He's so young and handsome!" And the old swans bowed their heads to him.

He suddenly felt shy and hid his head under his wings. He didn't know what to do—he was so happy, and yet not at all proud, because he had a good, honest heart. He thought of how he had been taunted and tormented, and now he heard all of them saying that he was the most beautiful of all beautiful birds. Even the lilacs bent their branches straight down into the water before him, and the sun beamed its golden warmth on him. He ruffled his feathers and lifted his slender neck, and from his heart he sang:

"I never dreamed of this much happiness when I was the ugly duckling!"

❧ The Little Mermaid ❧

FAR OUT IN THE OCEAN the water is as blue as the most beautiful cornflower and as clear as the purest crystal. But it is very deep—much deeper, in fact, than any anchor chain can sound. Many church steeples would have to be piled one on top of the other to reach from the bottom to the surface of the water. Down there live the sea folk.

Now you must not think that there is nothing but bare white sand down at the bottom. No, the strangest trees and plants grow there, with such pliant stems and leaves that at the slightest movement of the water they stir as if they are alive. All the big and little fishes glide in and out among their branches, as the birds do in the trees up above.

Where the ocean is deepest stands the Sea-King's palace. Its walls are made of coral, and the high arched windows of the clearest amber. The roof is made of mussel shells, which open and close in the current. It is very beautiful, for each of them is filled with gleaming pearls, any one of which would make a jewel fit for a queen's crown.

The Sea-King had been a widower for many years, but his old mother kept house for him. She was a clever woman, but very vain and proud of her noble rank, so she wore twelve oysters on her tail, while other nobles were only allowed to wear six. In other respects she deserved great praise, especially for her tender care of the little Sea-Princesses, her granddaughters. They were six lovely children, and the youngest was the most beautiful of all. Her skin was as clear and delicate as a rose petal, and her eyes as blue as the deepest sea, but, like all the others, she had no legs—her body ended in a fish-tail. All day long they used to play in the great halls of the palace, where living flowers grew out of the walls. When the large amber windows were thrown open, the fishes came swimming in to them, as the swallows fly in to us when we open our windows. But the fishes swam right up to the little Princesses, and ate out of their hands, and let themselves be petted and stroked.

In front of the palace was a large garden, in which bright red and dark blue trees were growing. The fruit glittered like gold, and the flowers looked like flames of fire, with their ever-moving stems and leaves. The ground was covered with the finest sand, as blue as burning brimstone. A strange blue light shone over everything, so that one could imagine oneself to be high up in the air, with the blue sky above and below, rather than at the bottom of the sea. When the sea was calm one could see the sun. It looked like a huge purple flower, from whose centre the light streamed forth.

Each of the little Princesses had her own place in the garden, where she could dig and plant as she pleased. One gave her flower bed the shape of a whale; another preferred to make hers like a little mermaid; but the youngest made hers as round as the sun, and only had flowers that shone red like it. She was a strange child, quiet and thoughtful. While her sisters made a great display of all sorts of curious objects that they found from wrecked ships, she only loved her rose-red flowers, like the sun above, and a beautiful marble statue of a handsome boy carved out of clear white stone, which had sunk from some wreck to the bottom of the sea. She had

planted by the statue a rose-coloured weeping willow, which grew well, with its fresh branches arching over it, down to the blue sand, and casting a violet shadow that moved to and fro like the branches, so that it looked as if the top of the tree and the roots were playing at kissing each other.

Nothing gave her more pleasure than to hear stories about the world of men above. She made her old grandmother tell her all she knew about ships and towns, people and animals. It seemed strangely beautiful to her that on earth the flowers were fragrant, for at the bottom of the sea they have no scent; that the woods were green, and that the fish which one saw there among the branches could sing so loudly and beautifully that it was a delight to hear them. The grandmother called the little birds fishes; otherwise her granddaughter would not have understood her, for they had never seen a bird.

"When you are fifteen years old," said the grandmother, "you will be allowed to go up to the surface of the sea and sit on the rocks in the moonlight, and see the big ships sail by. Then you will also see the forests and towns."

The following year one of the sisters would be fifteen; but the others—well, the sisters were each one year younger than the other; so the youngest had to wait fully five years before she could come up from the bottom of the sea and see what things were like on the earth above. But each promised to tell her sisters what she had seen and liked best on her first day, for their grandmother could not tell them enough—there were so many things they wanted to know.

None of them, however, longed so much to go up as the youngest, who had the longest time to wait, and was so quiet and thoughtful. Many a night she stood at the open window and looked up through the dark blue water, where the fishes splashed with their fins and tails. She could see the moon and the stars, which only shone faintly, but looked much bigger through the water than we see them. When something like a dark cloud passed under them, and hid them for a while, she knew it was either a whale swimming overhead or a ship with many people, who had no idea that a lovely little mermaid was standing below stretching out her white hands towards the keel of their ship.

The eldest Princess was now fifteen years old, and was allowed to rise to the surface of the sea. When she came back she had hundreds of things to tell: but what pleased her most, she said, was to lie in the moonlight on a sandbank, in the calm sea, and to see near the coast the big town where the lights twinkled like hundreds of stars; to hear the music and the noise and bustle of carriages and people, and to see the many church towers and spires and listen to the ringing of the bells.

Oh, how the youngest sister listened to all this! And when, later in the evening, she again stood at the open window, looking up through the dark blue water, she thought of the big town, with all its bustle and noise, and imagined that she too could hear the church bells ringing, even down where she was.

The next year the second sister was allowed to go up to the surface and swim about as she pleased. She came up just as the sun was setting, and this, she thought, was the most beautiful sight of all. The whole sky was like gold, she said, and the clouds—well, she could not find words to describe their beauty. Rose and violet, they sailed by over her head. But, even swifter than the clouds, a flock of wild swans, like a long white veil, flew across the water towards the sun. She followed them, but the sun sank, and the rosy gleam faded from the clouds and the sea.

The following year the third sister went up. She was the boldest of them all, and she swam up a broad river that flowed into the sea. She saw beautiful green hills covered with vines, and houses and castles peeped out from magnificent forests. She heard the birds sing, and the sun shone so warmly that she often had to dive under the water to cool her burning face. In a little creek she came across a whole flock of little children, who were quite naked and splashed about in the water. She wanted to play with them, but they were frightened and ran away. Then a little black animal—it was a dog, but she had never seen a dog before—came out and barked so ferociously at her that she became frightened and swam quickly back to the open sea. But she could never forget the beautiful forests, the green hills, and the lovely children, who could swim even though they had no fishtails.

The fourth sister was not so daring. She stayed far out in the open sea, and said that that was the loveliest place of all. There, she said, one could see for many miles around, and the sky above was like a great glass dome. She saw ships, but far away, and they looked to her like seagulls. The playful dolphins, she said, turned somersaults, and the big whales spewed out seawater through their spouts, as if a hundred fountains were playing all around her.

Now the fifth sister's turn came, and, as her birthday was in winter, she saw things on her first visit that the other sisters had not. The sea looked quite green; huge icebergs floated around her— they were like pearls, she said, and yet were much higher than the church steeples built by men. They were the strangest shapes and glittered like diamonds. She sat on one of the biggest, and all the passing sailors were terrified when they saw her sitting there, with the wind playing with her long hair. Towards evening the sky became overcast with black clouds; there was thunder and lightning, and the dark waves lifted up the big blocks of ice, which shone in each flash of lightning. On all the ships the sails were furled, and the men were filled with anxiety and terror. But she sat quietly on her floating iceberg and watched the blue lightning dart in zigzags into the foaming sea.

The first time each one of the sisters came to the surface all the new and beautiful things she saw charmed her. But now, when as grown-up girls they were allowed to come up whenever they liked, they soon ceased to marvel at the upper world and longed for their home; and after a month they said that after all it really was best down below, where one felt at home. On many an evening the five sisters would rise to the surface of the sea, arm in arm. They had beautiful voices, far finer than those of any human being; and when a storm was brewing, and they thought that some ships might be wrecked, they swam in front of them, singing so beautifully of how lovely it was at the bottom of the sea, and telling the sailors not to be afraid to come down to them. But the sailors could not understand the words and thought it was only the noise of the storm; and they never saw the wonders below, for when the ship went down they were drowned, and were dead when they came to the Sea-King's palace.

When her sisters went up arm in arm to the top of the sea there stood the little sister, all alone, looking after them, and feeling as if she wanted to cry. But mermaids have no tears, and so they suffer all the more.

"Oh, if I were only fifteen!" she said. "I know how much I shall love the world above, and the people who live in it."

At last she reached her fifteenth birthday.

"Well, now we have you off our hands," said her grandmother, the old dowager queen. "Come now! Let me dress you like your sisters!" She put a wreath of white lilies in her hair, but every petal of the flowers was half a pearl; and the old lady put eight big oysters on the Princess's tail, to show her high rank.

"But it hurts!" said the little mermaid.

"Yes, but one must suffer to be beautiful," said the old lady.

Oh, how gladly the little Princess would have taken off all her ornaments and the heavy wreath! The red flowers in her garden would have suited her much better, but she dared not make any change now. "Good-bye!" she said, and rose as lightly as a bubble through the water.

The sun had just set when she lifted her head out of the water, but the clouds gleamed with red and gold, and the evening star shone brightly in the rosy sky. The air was mild and fresh, and the sea as calm as glass. Near her lay a big ship with three masts. Only one sail was set, as not a breath of wind was stirring, and the sailors were sitting about on deck and in the rigging. There was music and singing on board, and when it grew dark many hundreds of coloured lamps were lighted, and it looked as if the flags of all nations were floating in the air. The little mermaid swam close to the cabin windows, and when the waves lifted her up she could see through the clear panes many richly dressed people. But the handsomest of

them all was the young Prince, with large black eyes. He could not have been more than sixteen. In fact, it was his birthday that was being celebrated. The sailors were dancing on deck, and when the young Prince came out hundreds of rockets rose into the air, making the night as bright as day, so that the little mermaid was frightened, and dived underwater. But soon she raised her head again, and then it seemed to her as if all the stars of heaven were falling down upon her. Never had she seen such fireworks! Great suns whirled around, wondrous fiery fish flew through the blue air, and everything was reflected in the clear, calm sea. The ship was so brilliantly lit up that one could see everything distinctly, even to the smallest rope, and the people still better. Oh, how handsome the young Prince was! He shook hands with the people and smiled graciously, while the music drifted through the starry night.

It grew very late, but the little mermaid could not tear her eyes away from the ship and the handsome Prince. The coloured lamps were put out, no more rockets were sent up nor cannons fired. But deep down in the sea was a strange moaning and murmuring, and the little mermaid sitting on the waves was rocked up and down, so that she could look into the cabin. Soon the ship began to move faster, as one sail after another was unfurled. Then the waves rose higher and higher, dark clouds gathered, and flashes of lightning were seen in the distance. Oh, what a terrible storm was brewing! Then the sailors reefed all the sails, and the big ship plunged wildly through the raging sea. The waves rose as high as great black mountains, as if they would dash over the masts, but the ship dived like a swan between them, and then was carried up again to their towering crests. The little mermaid thought this was great fun, but not the sailors. The ship creaked and groaned, her strong timbers gave way under the weight of the huge waves, the sea broke over her; the mainmast snapped in two, like a reed; and the ship heeled over on her side while the water rushed into her hold.

The little mermaid realized that the crew was in danger. She herself had to be careful of the beams and planks floating about in the water. For a moment it was so dark that nothing could be seen, but then flashes of lightning made everything visible, and she could see all on board. The little mermaid looked for the young Prince, and as the ship broke up she saw him sinking into the depths of the sea. At first she was very pleased, for now he would come down and live with her; but then she remembered that men cannot live in the water, and only if he were dead could he come to her father's palace. No, no, he must not die! Heedless of the beams and planks floating on the water, which could have crushed her, she dived down into the water and came up again in the waves, searching for the Prince. At last she found him. His strength was failing him, and he could hardly swim any longer in the raging sea. His arms and legs began to grow numb, and his beautiful eyes closed. He would certainly have died if the little mermaid had not come to his aid. She held his head above water and let the waves carry them where they would.

Next morning the storm was over, but not a plank of the ship was to be seen anywhere. The sun rose red and brilliant out of the water and seemed to bring new life to the Prince's cheeks, but his eyes remained closed. The little mermaid kissed his beautiful high forehead, and smoothed back his wet hair. She thought he looked very much like the white marble statue in her little garden. She kissed him again and again, and prayed that he might live.

Then she saw before her eyes the mainland with its high, blue mountains on whose summits snow was glistening, so that they looked like swans. Along the shore were beautiful green woods, and in front of them stood a church or convent—she did not know which, but it was some sort of building. Lemon trees and orange trees grew in the garden, and before the gate stood lofty palm trees. The sea formed a little bay here and was quite calm, though very deep. She swam straight to the cliffs, where the fine white sand had been washed ashore, and laid the handsome Prince on the sand, taking care that his head should lie in the warm sunshine.

Then all the bells began to ring in the big white building, and many young girls came out into the garden. The little mermaid swam out and hid behind some rocks, covering her hair and breast with sea foam, to make sure no one could see her face, and from there she watched to see who would come to find the poor Prince.

Before long a young girl came to the spot where he lay. At first she seemed very frightened, but only for a moment, then she called to some of the others. The little mermaid saw that the Prince came back to life, and smiled at all who stood around him. But he did not smile at her, for he did not know who had saved him. She was very sad; and when they had taken him into the big building, she dived down into the water and went back to her father's palace.

She had always been silent and thoughtful, and now she became even more so. Her sisters asked her what she had seen up above for the first time, but she told them nothing. Many a morning and many an evening she went back to the place where she had left the Prince. She saw how the fruit in the garden ripened and was gathered, and how the snow melted on the high mountains, but she never saw the Prince, and each time she returned home she was more unhappy than before.

Her only comfort was to sit in her little garden and put her arms around the marble figure which was so like the Prince. She no longer looked after her flowers. Her garden became a wilderness; the plants straggled over the paths and twined their long stalks and leaves around the branches of the trees, so that it became quite dark and gloomy there.

At last she could bear it no longer, and confided her troubles to one of her sisters, who, of course, told the others. These and a few other mermaids, who also told their intimate friends, were the only people who were in on the secret. One of them knew who the Prince was. She too had watched the festivities on board the ship, and could tell them where his kingdom lay.

"Come, little sister!" said the other Princesses, and linking arms, they rose to the surface of the sea, to where the Prince's palace stood. It was built of pale yellow stone, and had broad marble staircases, one of which reached right down to the sea. Magnificent gilt cupolas surmounted the roof, and in the colonnades, which ran all around the building, stood lifelike marble statues. Through the clear panes of the high windows could be seen stately halls, hung with costly silk curtains and beautiful tapestries, and on all the walls were beautiful paintings. In the centre of the largest hall a big fountain was playing. Its jets rose as high as the glass dome in the ceiling, through which the sun shone on the water and on the lovely plants that grew in the great basin.

Now she knew where he lived, and many an evening and many

a night she returned there. She swam much closer to the shore than any of the others had ventured, and she even went up the narrow channel under the magnificent marble balcony that cast a long shadow over the water. There she would sit and gaze at the young Prince, who thought that he was all alone in the bright moonlight.

Many an evening she saw him sailing in his stately boat, with music on board and flags waving. She watched from behind the green rushes, and when the wind caught her long silvery white veil, and people saw it, they thought it was only a swan spreading its wings. At night, when the fishermen were out casting their nets by lamplight, she heard them say many kind things about the Prince, and she was glad that she had saved his life when he was drifting half-dead on the waves. She remembered how heavily his head had lain upon her breast, and how lovingly she had kissed him, but he knew nothing of this, and did not even see her in his dreams.

Daily her love for human beings increased, and more and more she longed to be able to live among them, for their world seemed to her so much bigger than hers. They could sail over the sea in great ships and climb mountains higher than the clouds, and the lands they owned stretched out, in woods and fields, farther than her eyes could see. There were still so many things she wanted to know about, and as her sisters could not answer all her questions, she asked her grandmother, who knew the upper world very well, and rightly called it "the countries above the sea."

"If human beings are not drowned," asked the little mermaid, "can they live forever? Don't they die as we do down here in the sea?"

"Yes," said the old lady, "they also die, and their life is even shorter than ours. We can live to be three hundred, but when we cease to exist we are turned into foam on the water, and do not even have a grave down here among our loved ones. We do not have immortal souls, and can never live again. We are like the green rushes, which, when once cut down, can never grow again. Human beings, however, have a soul that lives forever, even after the body has turned to dust. It rises through the clear air up to the shining stars. As we rise out of the water and see all the countries of the earth, so they rise to unknown, beautiful regions which we shall never see."

"Why don't we also have an immortal soul?" said the little mermaid sorrowfully. "I would gladly give all the hundreds of years I have yet to live if I could only be a human being for one day, and afterwards have a share in the heavenly kingdom."

"You must not think of that," said the old lady. "We are much happier and better off than the human beings up there."

"So I must die, and float as foam on the sea, and never hear the music of the waves or see the beautiful flowers and the red sun! Is there nothing I can do to win an immortal soul?"

"No," said the grandmother. "Only if a man loved you so much that you were dearer to him than father or mother, and if he clung to you with all his heart and all his love, and let the priest place his right hand in yours, with the promise to be faithful to you here and for all eternity—then would his soul flow into your body, and you would receive a share in the happiness of mankind. He would give you a soul and still keep his own. But that can never happen! What is thought most beautiful here below, your fishtail, they would consider ugly on earth—they do not know any better. Up there one must have two clumsy props, which they call legs, in order to be beautiful."

The little mermaid sighed and looked sadly at her fishtail.

"Let us be happy!" said the old lady. "Let us hop and skip through the three hundred years of our life! That is surely long enough! And afterwards we can rest all the better in our graves. This evening there is to be a Court ball."

It was a magnificent sight, one such has never been seen on earth. The walls and ceiling of the big ballroom were of thick but transparent glass. Several hundred huge mussel shells, some red and others green as grass, stood in rows down the sides, holding blue flames, which illuminated the whole room and shone through the walls, so that the sea outside was brightly lit up. One could see countless fish, both big and small, swimming outside the glass walls; some with gleaming purple scales and others glittering like silver and gold. Through the middle of the ballroom flowed a broad stream, in which the mermen and mermaids danced to their own beautiful singing. No human beings have such lovely voices. The little mermaid sang most sweetly of all, and they all applauded her. For a moment she felt joyful at heart at the thought that she had the most beautiful voice on land or in the sea. But soon her thoughts returned to the world above, for she could not forget the handsome Prince and her sorrow at not possessing an immortal soul like his. So she stole out of her father's palace, while inside joy and merriment reigned, and sat sorrowfully in her little garden.

Suddenly she heard the sound of a horn through the water, and thought: "Now he is sailing above, he whom I love more than father or mother, and into whose hands I would entrust my life's happiness. I would risk anything to win him and an immortal soul. While my sisters are dancing in my father's palace I will go to the sea witch, whom I have always feared so much. Perhaps she may be able to give me advice and help."

Then the little mermaid left her garden, and went out towards the roaring whirlpools where the witch lived. She had never been that way before: no flowers, no seaweed even, were growing there— only bare, gray sand stretching to the whirlpools, where the currents swirled around like rushing mill wheels, dragging everything with it down into the depths. She had to pass through these dreadful whirlpools to reach the witch's territory. For a long way the only path led over hot bubbling mud, that the witch called the peat bog. Behind it her house stood, in a strange forest, for all the trees and bushes were polyps—half-animal and half-plant—which looked like hundred-headed snakes growing out of the ground. The branches had slimy arms with fingers like wriggling worms, and they moved joint by joint from the root to the topmost branch. Everything that they could lay hold of in the sea they grabbed and held fast, and never let it go again. The little mermaid stopped timidly in front of them. Her heart was pounding with fear, and she almost turned back. But then she thought of the Prince and of man's immortal soul, and took courage. She twisted her long flowing hair around her head, in case the polyps should try to seize her by it, and, crossing her hands on her breast, darted through the water as fast as a fish, right past the hideous polyps, who stretched out their writhing arms and fingers after her. She saw that each one of them had seized something, and held it tightly with hundreds of little arms like bands of iron. The bleached bones of men who had perished at sea and sunk into the depths were tightly grasped in the arms of some, while others clutched ships' rudders and sea chests, skeletons of land animals, and—the most terrifying sight of all to her—a little mermaid whom they had caught and strangled.

She came to a big slimy place in the forest, where big, fat water snakes were writhing about, showing their ugly yellow bellies. In the middle of this marsh stood a house built of the white bones of shipwrecked men, and there sat the sea witch, letting a toad eat out of her mouth, as we would feed a canary with sugar. The ugly, fat water snakes she called her little chickens, and allowed them to crawl all over her hideous bosom.

"I know exactly what you want!" said the sea witch. "It is stupid of you! But you shall have your way, for it is sure to bring you misfortune, my pretty Princess! You want to get rid of your fishtail and have, instead, two stumps that human beings use for walking, so that the young Prince may fall in love with you, and you may win him and an immortal soul!" As she said this the old witch laughed so loudly and horribly that the toad and the snakes fell to the ground, where they lay wriggling. "You have come just in time," said the witch, "for if you had come after sunrise tomorrow I would not have been able to help you for another year. I will make you a potion, and before sunrise you must swim ashore and sit on the beach and drink it. Then your tail will split in two and shrink into what human beings call legs. But I warn you it will hurt, as if a sharp sword were running through you. Everyone who sees you will say that you are the most beautiful child they have ever seen. You will keep your gracefulness, and no dancer will be able to move as lightly as you. But every step you take will be as painful as treading on a sharp knife. Are you willing to suffer all this, and shall I help you?"

"Yes," said the little mermaid in a trembling voice, and she thought of the Prince and the immortal soul.

"But remember!" said the witch. "When once you have taken the human form you can never become a mermaid again. You will never again be able to dive down through the water to your sisters and your father's palace. And if you fail to win the Prince's love, so that for your sake he will forget father and mother, and cling to you with body and soul, and make the priest join your hands as man and wife, you will not be given an immortal soul. On the first morning after he has married another, your heart will break, and you will turn into foam on the water."

"I will do it," said the little mermaid, as pale as death.

"But you must pay me," said the witch, "and it is not a trifle I ask. You have the most beautiful voice of all who live at the bottom of the sea, and you probably think you can charm the Prince with it—but this voice you must give to me. I must have the best thing you possess in return for my precious drink, for I have to give you my own blood in it, so that the drink may be as sharp as a two-edged sword."

"But if you take away my voice," said the little mermaid, "what have I got left?"

"Your lovely figure," said the witch, "your grace of movement, and your eloquent eyes! With these you can surely capture a human heart. Well, have you lost your courage? Put out your little tongue, so that I may cut it off in payment, and you shall have my magic potion."

"Go ahead," said the little mermaid, and the witch put her cauldron on the fire to prepare the magic drink. "Cleanliness is a good thing," she said, and scoured the cauldron with snakes, which she had tied into a bundle. Then she pricked her breast and let her black blood drip into it, and the steam rose up in the weirdest shapes, so that the little mermaid was frightened and horrified. Every moment the witch threw some new ingredient into the cauldron, and when it boiled the sound was like a crocodile weeping. At last the drink was ready, and it looked like the purest water.

"Here it is!" said the witch, and she cut off the little mermaid's tongue, so that now she was dumb and could neither sing nor speak. "If the polyps should catch hold of you on your way back through my wood," said the witch, "you need only throw one drop of this potion over them, and their arms and fingers will break into a thousand pieces!"

The little mermaid had no need to do this, however, for the polyps shrank back from her in terror at the sight of the sparkling drink, which gleamed in her hand like a glittering star. So she made her way quickly through the forest and the bog and the roaring whirlpools. She could see her father's palace: in the ballroom the lamps were all out and everyone was asleep, but she dared not go in to see them, now that she was dumb and about to leave them forever. She felt as if her heart would break with sorrow. She stole into the garden, took a flower from each of her sisters' flower beds, blew a thousand kisses to the palace, and then swam up through the dark blue sea.

The sun had not yet risen when she came in sight of the Prince's palace and reached the magnificent marble steps. The moon was shining bright and clear. The little mermaid drank the sharp, burning draught, and it felt as if a two-edged sword went through her tender body; she fainted, and lay as if dead.

When the sun shone over the sea she awoke, and felt a stabbing pain; but there before her stood the beautiful young Prince. He fixed his black eyes on her, so that she cast hers down and saw that her fishtail had disappeared, and that she now had the prettiest little white legs that any girl could wish for. She was quite naked, though, so she wrapped herself in her long, thick hair. The Prince asked her who she was and how she came to be there, and she looked at him tenderly and sadly with her deep blue eyes, for she could not speak. Then he took her by the hand and led her into the palace. Every step she took, as the witch had warned, was like walking on pointed needles and sharp knives, but she bore it gladly, and walked as lightly as a soap bubble by the side of the Prince, who, with all the others, admired her graceful movement.

They dressed her in costly silk and muslin, and she was the greatest beauty in the palace; but she was dumb, and unable either to sing or speak. Beautiful slaves, dressed in silk and gold, came to sing before the Prince and his royal parents. One of them sang better than all the rest, and the Prince clapped his hands and smiled at her. Then the little mermaid grew sad, for she knew that she had been able to sing far more beautifully; and she thought: "Oh, if only he knew that I have given away my voice for ever to be with him!"

Now the slaves began to dance light, graceful dances to the loveliest music; and then the little mermaid lifted her beautiful white arms, rose on her toes, and glided across the floor, dancing as no one had ever danced before. At every movement her beauty seemed

to grow, and her eyes spoke more deeply to the heart than the songs of the slave girls. Everyone was charmed by her, especially the Prince, who called her his little foundling, and she danced again and again, although every time her feet touched the ground she felt as if she were treading on sharp knives. The Prince said that she should always be near him, and let her sleep on a velvet cushion just outside his door.

He had a page's dress made for her, so that she could ride with him. They rode through sweet-smelling woods, where the green branches brushed her shoulders and the little birds sang among the fresh leaves. With the Prince she climbed the high mountains, and, though her tender feet bled so that all could see it, she smiled and followed him, till they saw the clouds sailing beneath them, like a flock of birds flying to foreign lands.

At home, in the Prince's palace, when all the others were asleep at night, she would go out onto the broad marble steps. It cooled her burning feet to stand in the cold seawater, and then she thought of those she had left down below in the deep.

One night her sisters came up arm in arm, singing sorrowfully as they swam through the water, and she beckoned to them, and they recognized her and told her how sad she had made them all. After that they came to see her every night, and one night she saw, far out to sea, her old grandmother, who had not been up to the surface for many, many years, and the Sea-King, with his crown on his head. They stretched out their hands towards her, but did not venture as close to land as her sisters.

Day by day the Prince grew fonder of her. He loved her as one would love a good, sweet child, but it never crossed his mind to make her his Queen. And yet his wife she must be, or she could not win an immortal soul, and on his wedding morning she would turn into foam on the sea.

"Don't you love me more than all of them?" the little mermaid's eyes seemed to say when the Prince took her in his arms and kissed her beautiful forehead.

"Yes, you are dearest to me," he said, "for you have the best heart of them all. You are the most devoted to me, and you are like a young girl whom I once saw, but whom I fear I shall never meet again. I was on a ship that was wrecked, and the waves washed me ashore near a holy temple where several young maidens were serving in attendance. The youngest of them found me on the beach and saved my life. I only saw her twice. She is the only girl in the world I could love, but you are very much like her, and you almost drive her image from my heart. She belongs to the holy temple, and so by good fortune you have been sent to me, and we shall never part."

"Alas! He doesn't know it was I who saved his life!" thought the little mermaid. "I carried him across the sea to the wood where the temple stands, and I was hidden in the foam, watching to see if anyone would come to him. I saw the beautiful girl whom he loves better than me." She sighed deeply, for she could not weep. "The girl belongs to the holy temple, he says. She will never come out into the world, and they will never meet again. But I am with him and see him every day. I will care for him, love him, and give up my life for him."

But soon the rumour spread that the Prince was to marry the beautiful daughter of a neighbouring King, and that that was why they were fitting up such a magnificent ship. The Prince is going to visit the neighbouring King's country, they said, but everyone knows he is really going to see his daughter. A large suite was to accompany him. The little mermaid shook her head and smiled, for she knew the Prince's thoughts much better than the others. "I must go," he said to her. "I must see the beautiful Princess, for my parents wish it; but they will not force me to bring her home as my bride. I cannot love her: she will not be like the beautiful girl in the temple whom you are like. If one day I were to choose a bride I would rather have you, my dumb foundling with the eloquent eyes." And he kissed her red lips, and played with her long hair, and laid his head on her heart, so that she began to dream of human happiness and an immortal soul.

"You are surely not afraid of the sea, my silent child?" he said to her, when they were standing on board the stately ship that was to carry him to the neighbouring King's country. He told her of the storm and of the calm, of the strange fish in the deep, and of the marvellous things that divers had seen down there, and she smiled at his words, for she knew more about the things at the bottom of the sea than anyone on earth.

At night, in the bright moonlight, when everyone was asleep except the man at the helm, she sat by the ship's rail, gazing down into the clear water, and thought she could see her father's palace, and her grandmother, with her silver crown on her head, looking up through the swirling currents at the ship's keel. Then her sisters came up out of the water, looking sorrowfully at her and wringing their white hands. She beckoned to them, and smiled, and wanted to tell them that she was well and happy, but a cabin boy came up to her, and her sisters dived under, so that he thought it was just foam on the sea.

The next morning the ship reached the harbour of the neighbouring King's beautiful city. All the church bells were ringing, and from the high towers trumpets sounded, while soldiers paraded with flying colours and glittering bayonets. Every day there were festivities; balls and receptions followed one another, but the Princess had not yet arrived. She was in a holy convent far away, they said, where she was learning every royal virtue. At last she came. The little mermaid was anxious to see her beauty, and she had to admit that she had never seen anyone lovelier. Her skin was clear and delicate, and behind her long dark lashes smiled a pair of deep blue, loyal eyes.

"You are she!" said the Prince. "She who saved me when I lay almost dead on the shore!" And he clasped his blushing bride in his arms.

"Oh, I am too happy!" he said to the little mermaid. "My greatest wish, which I have never dared hope for, has come true. You will rejoice at my happiness, for you love me more than them all." The little mermaid kissed his hand, and felt as if her heart was already breaking: his wedding morning, she knew, would bring her death, and she would turn into foam on the sea.

The church bells pealed and heralds rode through the streets announcing the betrothal. On all the altars scented oil was burning in costly silver lamps. The priests swung their censers, and the bride and bridegroom joined hands and received the bishop's blessing. The little mermaid, dressed in silk and gold, stood holding the bride's train, but her ears did not hear the joyous music, and her eyes saw nothing of the sacred ceremony—she was thinking of her death, and of all that she had lost in this world.

That same evening the bride and bridegroom came on board the ship; cannons thundered, flags were waved, and in the middle of the ship was erected a royal tent of purple and gold, with the most magnificent couch, where the bridal pair were to rest through the still, cool night.

The sails swelled in the wind, and the ship glided smoothly and almost without motion over the clear sea. When it grew dark coloured lamps were lighted, and the sailors danced merrily on deck. The little mermaid could not help thinking of the first time she had risen to the surface and had seen the same splendour and revelry. She threw herself among the dancers, darting and turning as a swallow turns when it is pursued, and they all applauded her, for she had never danced so beautifully before. It was like sharp knives cutting her tender feet, but she did not feel it, for the pain in her heart was much greater. She knew that it was the last evening that she would be with him—him for whom she had left her family and her home, sacrificed her lovely voice, and daily suffered endless pain, of which he knew nothing. It was the last night that she would breathe the same air as he, and see the deep sea and the starry sky. An eternal, dreamless night was waiting for her who had no soul and could not win one. On board the ship the merrymaking lasted till long past midnight, and she laughed and danced with the thought of death in her heart. The Prince kissed his beautiful bride, and she played with his dark hair, and arm in arm they retired to rest in the magnificent tent.

Everything grew quiet on board; only the steersman stood at the

helm. The little mermaid laid her white arms on the rail and looked towards the east for the rosy glimmer of dawn, for she knew that the first sunbeam would kill her.

Then she saw her sisters rising out of the waves; they were as pale as she was, and their beautiful hair no longer floated in the wind, for it had been cut off. "We have given it to the witch, to get her help, so that you will not die tonight. She has given us a knife: here it is. See how sharp it is! Before the sun rises you must thrust it into the Prince's heart, and when the warm blood sprinkles your feet they will grow together again into a fishtail. Then you will be a mermaid again, and you can come down with us into the sea, and live your three hundred years before you turn into sea foam. Hurry! For he or you must die before sunrise. Our old grandmother is so full of grief for you that her white hair has all fallen out, as ours fell under the witch's scissors. Kill the Prince and come back to us! Hurry! Do you see that red streak in the sky? In a few moments the sun will rise, and then you must die!" They gave a deep sigh and disappeared beneath the waves.

The little mermaid drew back the purple curtain of the tent and saw the lovely bride lying asleep with her head on the Prince's breast, and she bent down and kissed him on his beautiful forehead. She looked up at the sky, where the rosy glow was growing brighter and brighter, and then at the sharp knife, and again at the Prince, who murmured his bride's name in his dreams. Yes, she alone was in his thoughts, and for a moment the knife trembled in the little mermaid's hand. But suddenly she flung it far out into the waves: they shone red where the knife fell, so that it looked as if drops of blood were splashing up out of the water. Once more she looked with dimmed eyes at the Prince, then threw herself from the ship into the sea, and felt her body dissolving into foam.

Now the sun rose out of the sea and its rays fell with gentleness and warmth on the deathly cold sea foam, and the little mermaid felt no pain of death. She saw the bright sun and, floating above her, hundreds of beautiful transparent beings, through whom she could see the white sails of the ship and the red clouds in the sky. Their melodious voices were so ethereal that no human ear could hear them, just as no earthly eye could see them, and without wings they floated through the air. The little mermaid saw that she had a body like theirs and was slowly rising up out of the foam.

"Where am I going?" she asked, and her voice sounded like that of the other spirits—so ethereal that no earthly music was like it.

"To the daughters of the air," answered the others. "Mermaids have no immortal soul, and can never have one unless they win the love of a human being. Their eternal life must depend on the power of another. The daughters of the air have no immortal soul either, but by their own good deeds they can win one for themselves. We fly to the hot countries where the pestilent winds kill human beings, and we bring them cool breezes. We spread the fragrance of the flowers through the air, and bring life and healing. When for three hundred years we have striven to do all the good we can, we are given an immortal soul and share the eternal happiness of mankind. You, poor little mermaid, have struggled with all your heart for the same goal, and have suffered and endured. Now you have risen to the spiritual world, and after three hundred years of good deeds you can win an immortal soul for yourself."

And the little mermaid lifted her eyes to the sun, and for the first time she felt tears in them.

On the ship there was life and noise once more. She saw the Prince and his beautiful bride looking for her, and gazing sadly at the gleaming foam, as if they knew that she had thrown herself into the waves. Unseen, she kissed the bride's forehead and smiled at the Prince. Then she rose with the other children of the air up to the rosy clouds that sailed across the sky.

"In three hundred years we shall float like this into the kingdom of God!"

"But we may get there sooner!" whispered one of them. "Unseen, we fly into houses where there are children, and for every day that we find a good child who gives its parents joy and deserves their love, God shortens our time of probation. The child does not know when we fly through the room, and if we smile at his goodness one of the three hundred years is taken off. But if we see a naughty and wicked child, we shed tears of sorrow, and every tear adds a day to our time of probation."